IF THESE

STREETS

COULD TALK

To Ivy: I hope you enjoy
my story

Gino Arroyo

Cover by: Will Moore
Printed by: RJ Communications
Printed in the United States of America

ISBN:978-1-4675-5646-0
TXul-280-665

www.ginoarroyopublishing.com

In Loving Memory of My Beloved Mother

Kathryn Arroyo-Drake

Table Of Contents

If These Streets Could Talk

He Saved Me

He saved me.

He knew *He* would save me when *He* knit me together in the depths of my Mother's womb.

He knew the path I would follow knowing me personally from each and every hair on my head individually.

He saved me growing up through some of the hard times without food or sometime heat or sometime sleep through the struggle and agony of defeat. *He* saved me.

He saved me from these mean streets when I was drug using selling and stealin, wheelin and dealin. And when I avoided going to jail because of a so called friend squealin. *He* saved me.

He saved me from the crack and the crack heads the drugs and the drug raids and that beautiful girl I wanted so bad but couldn't have to later find out she had AIDS. *He* save me when the bullets came flying my way and because of *H*im I got out of the way. And when I was cornered *He* made a way out of no way. And that's the only reason why I'm here today is because *He* saved Me.

He Saved me because he loves me and *He* teaches me to love others not superficially but unconditionally.

He even loved me when I didn't love myself and I adore him for what he has done. *He* is the true meaning of the phrase, " like Father like Son". *He* saved me.

Gino Arroyo

If These Streets Could Talk

Ch 1 Old School

"Crack!"

Out of nowhere something hit me in my right ear so hard that my sunglasses, hat, and book bag all flew off simultaneously. I stumbled a few feet and fell so hard into a parked car that my head print was indented into the passenger side door. I thought that a car had just hit me. I was dazed but still conscious.

As my vision became clearer I was able to focus on the object coming towards me. As my focus became clearer I saw that it was Craig, the dude's head that I had busted with a pipe a few days ago.

"Get the fuck up and take this ass whippin like a man!" He yelled coming towards me.

I saw two more of his boys across the street trying to get past the oncoming traffic to cross over to the other side to get me. That's when I shook off my semi-conscious state, stood to my feet, and took off running.

Everything happened so fast. Craig grabbed the back of my shirt but I tore away leaving him with a piece of my Izoid shirt in his right hand from the Barry Sanders back spin I put on him. I then shook his boys and at the same time avoided getting hit by another moving car.

As the G bus that runs down 56th St. was loading and unloading passengers on the corner of 56th and Market street, people looked startled as I ran past moving cars ducking punches as Craig and his hit squad tried to ambush me.

If These Streets Could Talk

As all of this was going on it gradually dawned on me where is Jones? Did he set me up? Did he run out on me? Why the hell isn't he running too?

The next thing I heard was…

"Move G move!" POW, POW POW. "Move!"

I looked across the street and Jones was running towards me shooting at Craig and his boys. People at the bus stop started screaming and running into stores and ducking behind parked cars for shelter. The bus that was loading passengers on and off the bus immediately closed the doors and rushed off.

"Kill them motherfuckers!" I yelled as I ducked too from Jones uncontrolled gun fire.

At that moment Jones was my hero because I knew those big dudes would have killed me if they got their hands on me.

Craig and his boys scattered like cockroaches in the kitchen when you turn on the lights at 3:00 am to get a glass of water.

Me and Jones heard police sirens from a distance so we ran towards the "W" which was only two blocks away.

We both ran straight to the first floor and told Case what had happened. I couldn't believe he actually thought it was funny.

"Well bighead you got your first experience of retaliation," He said while laughing. "You put your guard down after you cracked that boy's head and that was a major mistake. You thought that it was over since some time had passed. Well guess what? 'It ain't over until it's over. Unless you kill a nigga or beat his ass real bad, you have to constantly watch your back for the sneak attack."

Case grabbed me by my chin and spun my face around towards him to examine my ear.

"Man look at your ear. It looks like he hit you with a brick," he said still laughing.

7

If These Streets Could Talk

As my adrenalin level lowered, my pain level increased. My ear was really pounding with pain. The way my ear looked he must have been wearing a ring or something I thought.

I went over to the mirror and seen my right ear was twice the size as my left and was bleeding. My first thought was retaliation but then I thought to myself that if someone had busted my head the way I did Craig's, I would have reacted the same way.

Jones asked, "So what do you want to do, go down South Philly on a seek and destroy mission?"

I looked again in the mirror and thought for a second.

"Naw man, lets let it ride for now."

Then something else dawned on me.

"And by the way Jones, where in the hell did you get a real gun from?"

If These Streets Could Talk

Ch 2 West Philly

I know that God has had an angel protecting me all of my life and believe me, I have kept him busy. I was born Giovanni Manuel Pizarro. I got my last name Pizarro from my father who was Puerto Rican. My father doesn't have the average Puerto Rican characteristics and neither do I. He had very dark skin and a full head of course gray hair that he had since the age of sixteen. I too was dark brown skinned with course hair and a full nose.

I never understood why or how my father and my mother never lived together but managed to have four children. Maybe it was because my dad had nineteen kids spread out from Philadelphia to Puerto Rico. That's right, fourteen girls and five boys. And although my three sisters and I were his only American children, it didn't make much difference since he equally neglected to support us all equally, he was very selective of what he choose to do.

My mother wanted us to have a good education; that's why she sent us to Mequan Elementary School, (a predominately white private school in Mequan Pennsylvania). It cost $1,500 a year per child (mind you this was the 1970's and that was a lot of money for families). My mother got us unto Mequan through some kind of program for fatherless children. She made us lie to the director telling him that our father was dead so we could attend for free. I actually watched my mother take a cut onion out of a plastic bag that was in her pocketbook and put it up to her eyes to make her eyes tear before we met with the people from the grant board. The rich and wealthy used to donate money to the program as a tax write off. In those days, my mother was a strong believer in a good education. To her, "If it was white, it was right."

If These Streets Could Talk

Every since I was five years old going to Mequan Elementary School, a predominately white school, my angel has protected me from any harm or danger that came my way. Of my three sisters, I was the next to the youngest and let me tell you, it wasn't easy growing up with five woman in the house; The fifth being my grandmother who had lived with us since I was born. My grandmother couldn't read nor write. In her younger days down south, the oldest children were forced to work and help take care of their younger siblings. So while my mother cleaned doctor's and lawyer's houses for a living, my grandmother raised us and taught us every domesticated task that she knew. By the age of seven, I knew how to hand wash my clothes, hem my pants, iron, and cook small meals.

My mother really confused me when she talked to someone white. It was sort of scary as if she was a totally different person. Her facial expression would change and she would reveal the biggest brightest smile while using her extra proper vocabulary and soft-spoken voice. I called it her white face. I couldn't believe this was the same woman who drank at night and beat the hell out of me. She knew exactly when and how to put on her mask and she wore it well.

Oh yeah, beatings were a part of my life. My mom was what I called a functional alcoholic. She would work and handle all of her business during the day, but at night she would get her drink on. That was usually when the beatings occurred. Not to say that I didn't deserve some of the beatings because I was no saint, but it was the severity of the beatings that I couldn't understand. She would beat me with any and every object she could get her hands on: broomsticks, extension cords, and high heeled shoes. Once she pulled a leather whip out of nowhere and beat me like a blonde headed stepchild. In this day and time, the welts and bruises that were left on my body would have definitely been a case of child abuse, but in those days, it was just a good old fashion butt-whipping.

Going to Mequan also let me see both sides of the world. The school was beautiful. Mequan was huge and had greenery surrounding the campus as far as the eye could see. It had live animals like, sheep and goats, that we could feed and tend to, and on warm days, we would sit outside and have class outdoors in the grass. We would drink from live springs and we were shown how to eat plants and berries. We also referred to our teachers on a first name basis, which was unheard of in the public school system. Although my sisters and I were among the only few blacks in the entire school, we were never made to feel uncomfortable. The teachers there gave us all equal amounts of love and attention.

After a day in the land of make believe, we would take our school bus or car pool back to West Philadelphia where my real roots were. I loved my neighborhood in West Philadelphia. 56th & Walnut St. or the 'W' as we called it. Although my mother still had to scramble cleaning for others, my mom owned the only triplex building on the block surrounded by duplexes. It sat on the corner adjacent to a bar and a variety store. Each apartment was very large and spacious which was perfect since six of us lived there. Our building had a indoor fire escape which we would run up and down playing hide and seek. My mom never made much money off of her building since either family or friends utilized each apartment. She was very open hearted and had an open door policy. It was also the official meeting place for all of my friends.

Growing up on the 'W' was pure fun. Every Friday night my mother, Kathryn whose knick name was K.K., would throw the wildest parties in the basement of our building. Our basement had an outside entrance on the side of the building that gave it easy access, and my mother was very much respected in the neighborhood. Although she was short, light brown skinned with freckles, and a natural red head, she was one of the only female property owners around our way so a lot of people really admired that about her. On the weekends all of KK's friends from the neighborhood would come and eat, drink, dance, and gamble all night long. Once when I was seven years old there was a severe rainstorm that flooded our entire basement. I sat with my legs crossed Indian style on top of our jukebox and watched as all of the adults rolled up their pants, took off their shoes, and kept partying in the water while dancing to the sounds of Al Green, Marvin Gay, and Earth Wind and Fire. It was the best!

Unfortunately life on the "W" wasn't always a party. There wasn't always enough money around to take care of life's bare necessities. There were times when food was scarce and clothes were worn down, but worst than that was the winter. I recall not having heat one year sitting in the living room blowing steam from out of my mouth. At night, we would sleep fully clothed and in the morning KK would wake us up one at a time and take us to the kitchen where she would boil hot water and pour it in the kitchen sink so we could wash up before school. That year near Christmas, KK had to make a choice: celebrate with a tree and toys, or get the furnace fixed. My older sister Banita was sitting in the corner with her jaw shivering and blurted out, "whhhaaattt dododo youyouyou thhhiiinnnkkk?"

When I was about 9 years old, my oldest sister Rochelle had a boyfriend named Cashes Smith but his nick name was Case. Since Rochelle was the oldest, KK let her move in on the first floor of our building by herself and in time Case moved in with her. Case was big, black, and muscular with very dark skin and African features. He also had a big afro and one gold earring. Case couldn't read or write very well because he had very limited education but anything dealing with the streets, he mastered. One thing Case taught me in life is that common sense can take you further than any education, and Case had plenty common sense. There are a lot of people with college degrees and no common since.

Case's mother and father were killed in a drug deal gone bad when he was 12 years old and he has been on his own ever since. Let him tell it he was raised by wolves. He and Rochelle met at his aunt's house who wrote street numbers. Rochelle would go there to play the numbers for KK. Case was 20 years old and Rochelle was 16 and beautiful. She had big pretty eyes, pearly white teeth, and was full figured. She kind of resembled Thelma on "Good Times." I would get angry walking down the street with her because she would attract too much attention from older guys hooting and whistling at her.

Case treated Rochelle nice at first, as all men do in the beginning, You know, show them our representative then the real us comes out. As time went on, Case's street mentality started to surface and his true colors came out. He had a very bad temper and was easily angered. Case would hit and beat Rochelle at any given moment for any given reason. The sad thing about it was she would come home with a black eye and deny his abuse. She would tell KK that she got into a fight at school or she fell at cheerleader practice out of fear of more abuse. I never understood why Rochelle was so afraid of Case knowing that my father did time in prison for murder and made it very clear that he didn't have a problem going back to jail if it meant protecting one his children.

One thing I did admire about Case was his way of dress. He was always up on the latest styles and fashions, and he had a variety of everything. You would almost never see him in the same outfit twice. He talked a lot of slang and broken English always trying to convince people that he was from NY or Jamaica. Oh, and did I mention that he was also a professional liar? I don't mean little white lies. I mean it was like he had a degree in lieology. He could convince an atheist that there is a God. With my father not around much, he was the only male role model I had so he taught me the only thing that he knew. How to survive on the streets. He would constantly tell me, "If your not strong out here you'll get eaten alive.

Case was also a walking pharmacy. If it could get you high, he could get it for you. He sold every kind of drug ever made but his biggest profit maker was marijuana. He sold it and smoked it all day long.

On my eleventh birthday me and Case were sitting on my third floor porch looking over the balcony and as usual he was smoking a joint telling me one of his superman stories. When he finished telling me for the fourth time about when he got shot in the back with a shotgun (which I knew because the pellets were still embedded in his back) I asked him.

"Case, why do you smoke that stuff all of the time?"

He lied as usual,

"Because I have glaucoma. Plus it also helps my cataracts. Why, do you want to try some?" handing it to me.

"Yea let me try."

I took the joint and examined it noticing that the tip of it was wet from Case's large, always moist lips. I wiped off the tip of it with my finger, put it to my lips and inhaled. The smoke filled my lungs so quickly that I started gagging and coughing until I vomited. Case thought it was funny.

"Naw Big Head," using the name he used to call me, "like this."

If These Streets Could Talk

After I stopped gagging, I caught my breath composing myself. I watched closely as Case put the joint up to his lips and inhaled slowly. He held it in for a few seconds then blew out a huge cloud of smoke.

"Here, now do it like that. Take it in easy."

I took the joint and put it up to my lips and inhaled slowly. I held in the smoke and exhaled while passing it back to Case, this time without choking.

I looked at Case.

"How do you like that?"

"Alright Big Head be careful. That's not regular weed, it's Ty stick."

After not choking the second time I felt overly confident.

"Man, Ty stick my stick. Just give me back the joint," I said boastfully.

I gradually started to feel light headed and my body felt like I was moving in slow motion. Case gave me a strange look.

"You all right Big Head"?

I looked him dead in the eye and broke out into a hysterical laughter.

"Aww shit, this little nut is trippin."

Then he began to laugh too.

Before I knew it, we were both laughing so hard that tears were coming out of our eyes. I was rolling around on the porch holding my stomach but the funny thing was that we didn't even know why we were laughing.

After what felt like a half an hour of laughter Case realized it was about 5:00 pm so he told me to pull myself together before KK got home. Me and him we went into the kitchen and fried a couple of egg sandwiches. I didn't even like eggs but I remember it being the best egg sandwich that I had ever eaten in my life. (I think they call that the munchies).

At 5:30 pm we heard the door open. It was KK and my sisters, Rochelle, Banita, and Maria.

"Ok, get yourself together, and don't trip," he threatened me.

We greeted my family at the door and helped them bring in the groceries that they were carrying. My next to the oldest sister Banita who was always observant and curious looked at me suspiciously.

"Boy why are your eyes so red?"

I looked at her and then covered my eyes with one hand.

"Because the rays from your ugly face is making them sting."

I dropped the bags on the floor and broke back into laughter. I also broke the spaghetti sauce for that night's dinner and KK was furious. She started slapping me but I couldn't stop laughing. Then she took off her shoe and starting hitting me with it hard and although it hurt I couldn't stop laughing. She had to stop beating me because she started having an asthma attack. I'll get you later," she threatened as she grabbed her inhaler and breathed in the steroid medication. Case grabbed me by the collar.

"I'll take care of him KK."

He dragged me through our long apartment hallway from the dining room straight into the bathroom.

As I continued to giggle uncontrollably, he took me to the tub and held my head under some cold water almost drowning me.

"Stop man, I can't breath," I gasped trying to fight him off me.

"Yea it ain't so funny now is it? You gets no more wacky weed," he said throwing me to the floor.

He left me on the bathroom floor soaking wet. I was mad, but I have to admit that the ice cold water brought down my high.

If These Streets Could Talk

The next day, I went to Case's best friend Tommy's house who also sold weed. Tommy, like Case, was also a flashy dresser. Also since it was the Bruce Lee era, both of them practiced martial arts and were pretty good at it. The two of them would practice on each other with full contact sometimes really hurting each other but still remaining best friends. A little crazy if you ask me. When he answered the door he looked as if he just woke up. His nappy bush was matted on one side and he had dried up drool on one side of his mouth.

"Case wants me to get a nick (a five dollar bag of marijuana) from you."

He looked at me in disbelief then started scratching his nappy hair.

"Well then why didn't Case come and get it himself?"

"Look man don't interrogate me, I'm just the messenger. Are you going to sell it to me or what?"

"Don't raise your voice at me young boy."

He mugged me in the face with his large hands.

"Just give me the money."

Me and Tommy exchanged weed for money.

"If I find out you're lying I'm going to tell Case and after he finishes smacking you around I'm going to stomp you to death."

"Yea, whatever."

I just snatched the bag and ran down the steps happily with the weed in hand.

I ran straight to the corner store on the "W" and stood outside. From a distance I seen Jo staggering down the street.

"Yo Jo! You want to make a dollar?"

You dam right young blood, whatcha need?"

Jo was our neighborhood drunk; everybody had at least one. Joe would do almost anything for a buck. The sad thing is Jo use to own his own business until he got divorced and his wife took him to the cleaners leaving him broke, so he stayed drunk all of the time.

"Here's a dollar. Go in and buy me some Top Paper."

"Sure young blood, easiest dollar I ever made," he said stuffing the dollar bill in his sock.

When I got home I went into the bathroom and attempted to roll a joint. It didn't look as neat as Case's but it worked. I stuck my head out of the window and lit up.

I smoked about half of it then put it out and was immediately back in funny world. The feeling felt so good I just had to re-experience it.

I went into the kitchen and opened the refrigerator since the munchies were hitting me hard. There were some leftover green peas in a pot so I got two pieces of bread and poured the peas on the bread and smashed the bread together trying to contain the peas into a sandwich. Every time I bit my green pea sandwich peas would roll out of the side so I tried to catch them after every bite tossing them right back into my mouth. When I finally realized what I was doing, I started cracking up. I thought to myself, "damn I'm high."

At the time my grandmother walked into the kitchen. She was on the telephone talking away. My grandmother was always doing something around the house like cooking or cleaning or something. She would wash all of our clothes in the kitchen sink with a washboard and steaming hot water with her bare hands. It hurt just looking at her but our clothes were always cleaner then they would be if we put them in a washing machine. That wasn't old school. That was some slave stuff.

She was still on the phone, "Yeah girl, Deacon James asked me out to dinner with his old slew feet walkin like a penguin. Ha Ha Ha...."

I had noticed that my little sister Maria had left her Chinese rope (a rope consisting of several rubber bands knotted together) on the floor. As my grandmother was on the phone talking I tapped her on the shoulder and whispered to her, "Grandma hold this," handing her one side of the Chinese rope. She, not paying attention, so deep into her conversation, held the rubber band while I stretched it out as far as it could go and released it.

"Pop!"

"Ahhhh!"

She dropped the phone and chased me out the front door.

"You got to come home sooner or later!" She yelled waving a broomstick in the air as I ran away laughing.

If These Streets Could Talk

Ch 3 New Jersey

After accidentally setting our kitchen on fire while smoking a joint when I was 12, KK thought it best that she send me to live with my godmother and godfather in Pennsauken NJ. I totally opposed the idea of leaving all of my family and friends in Philly, but I was forced to go.

My godmother was in her early sixties, but the way she looked and carried herself you could never tell. She had very pale skin which she camouflaged so well with cosmetics that she applied to perfection. Her facial features would make it easy for one to believe that she was of Caucasian decent with her pointed nose, thin pink lips, and natural long red hair. At times, I believed she wanted people to think that she was white. She was very classy and sophisticated always wearing fine jewelry, very expensive clothing, and perfume that cost $100 an ounce (mind you this was in 1977). Although she was well spoken and well mannered, if you rubbed her the wrong way, you would receive a royal cursing out. How she and my godfather ever bonded always remained a mystery to me.

My godfather, on the other hand, was the complete opposite. He was an alcoholic and a kleptomaniac. Not a functional alcoholic like KK . I'm talking a real looser. He was always out of work, or he would get fired for being drunk on the job, being late and absent, or for stealing. And when I say he was a kleptomaniac, I don't use the word lightly. He really had a sickness. No matter where we went he would have to steal something. If we were at the supermarket he would come out of the store with his pants stuffed with T-bone steaks. If we were at somebody's house, he would ask to use their bathroom, and you could best believe that he was upstairs casing their bedroom. I've been around a lot of thieves in my life but he was scary. He would commit high-risk crimes like snatching a motorcycle from in front of a car dealership and running away with it while the salesman wasn't looking, or break into someone's home while they were still in it. He was so slick that he could swim without even getting wet. I never really liked him because I never knew what was going through his mind.

The New Jersey scenery was beautiful, but everything was moving too slow for my style of living. Even though my godmother had a beautiful home and supplied me with my own bedroom, which I never had in Philly, my own dog, a giant dark-grey French poodle named Cuddles, and all of the goodies that a kid could eat, it just wasn't the "W."

We lived in a mixed middle-class neighborhood where everyone was married with families and worked everyday. Most of the people were friendly respectable folks except for this one old storeowner named Mr. Max and his dog Sam. From his actions, I thought he was prejudiced against blacks and Hispanics, but in time I concluded that he just hated everyone. No matter how nice of an approach or greeting you gave him, he still was mean. "Good morning Mr. Max," I would say, and he would just look at you with those beady little eyes and shriveled up prune looking face and would just barely mumble a return greeting. We only patronized him because he owned the only variety store in our community.

Sam was some kind of black and white mixed mutt of a dog. Although Mr. Max knew that Sam was aggressive he would let him roam around in front of his store unleashed. He would bark at every customer that would enter the store.

Once I was walking Cuddles and Sam came out of nowhere and attacked him. Cuddles tried to fight back but he was a French poodle and no more. I tried to get Sam off of Cuddles but Sam kept attacking .

"Sam, get over here,!" Mr. Max yelled from out of the screen door of the store. Sam ran over to him as I was picking Cuddles up off of the ground. Mr. Max didn't even apologize. He just gave me that evil look and shut his door.

Cuddles was beat up pretty badly. I had to carry him all of the way home bleeding and whimpering. He had puncture wounds to his face and all around his body. I was in tears.

When I got home my godmother was sitting in the living room watching the news. I tried to sneak past her but she spun around in her recliner and saw blood all over me and Cuddles

"What did you do to Cuddles?" She yelled jumping up snatching him out of my hands.

"I didn't do anything. It was Sam; he came out of nowhere and attacked us!"

"Well you know better then to have him near that dog. Why did you take him to the store with you anyway?"

"I always take him with me when I go to the store."

"Well not anymore you won't!"

Now she too was crying and holding a whimpering Cuddles in her arms while walking up the stairs .

"I'm disgusted with you Giovanni! Go to your room and don't come out until I tell you to!"

She directed her attention back to Cuddles.

"Come on baby, Mommy is going to take good care of you.

My feelings were crushed. I couldn't believe she thought I would actually allow Cuddles to get mauled on purpose. I loved him just as much as she did, if not more.

If These Streets Could Talk

I was prepared to get a beating like I was accustomed to at home in Philly, but she just put me on punishment for a week telling me not to go outside. No beating. That was a first for me.

That night I convinced myself that it was time to put an end to Sam.

Case once showed me a way of getting rid of unwanted animals, so the next day before school, I took two hot dogs out of the freezer and hid them down in the basement behind the oil tank so they could thaw out.

The next day after school my godmother sent me around the corner to the drug store to pick up her prescription medication. She took medication everyday since she had everything from high blood pressure to diabetes to a bad heart. Maybe the 2 ½ packs of cigarettes she smoked everyday had a little to do with it.

While the old man behind the counter had his back turned and was babbling on about how the Nets beat the 76ers, since he knew I was from Philly, I reached around the counter and stole a hypodermic needle and slid it in my pocket.

When I got home I took the needle down the basement and gathered my ingredients. I took some rat poison pellets from under the sink and a spoon then ground them up in a bowl until they turned into a powder form. I then added a few ounces of bleach and ammonia in the bowl and slowly mixed it up. I recall getting a little light headed so I wrapped a tee shirt around my face to filter out some of the fumes. Then I took the hot dogs and injected them with my generic toxic mixture.

Late that night when my godparents were asleep, I snuck out of the house and headed to the back of the store where Sam stayed. As soon as he saw me he started barking and trying his best to jump over the fence to get a taste of me.

"Hey Sam old buddy, I got a treat for you," I whispered waving the toxic hot dogs in the air.

He jumped so high that he almost bit me trying to snatch them out of my hand. "There you go, eat it all up." I watched as he devoured my toxic-hot dogs.

I ran back home, snuck into the house, and crept into my bed with a smile on my face.

It's amazing how rigor mortis stiffens a body in just a few hours after death because the next morning poor old Sam was as stiff as a board. Mr. Max was holding him like a surf board as he stood in his back yard crying his eyes out. The neighbors all stood around trying to console him as they wondered who committed this hideous crime. He even got into a fight with his next-door neighbor accusing him for the death of his mutt.

The police ended up taking Mr. Max away in hand cuffs when he threatened to kill everyone in the neighborhood until somebody confessed to poisoning his dog. He eventually closed down his store and moved away leaving our neighborhood without a variety store. I didn't know killing his dog would have affected him the way that it did, but retaliation was a must. Although our neighborhood was minus a store, the streets were a lot safer without Sam around.

If These Streets Could Talk

Ch 4 Education Is Key

Going to school in NJ was mentally challenging. I was only in the 6th grade, but we were doing what appeared to be 8th-grade work, I could barely keep up. Our teacher Mr. Moore was a short, fat, balding on top white man with a potbelly and thick bifocal glasses. It always amazes me how when older white men start to bald on top, they take hair from one side of their head and flip it to the other side to hide the hole in their natural. But when black men start balding, they just cut it all off. Hmmm. Anyway, Mr. Moore made us memorize a little saying he had:

"Good Better Best, Let Us Not Rest, Until Our Good Is Better, And Our Better Is Best."

I'll never forget it because he made us live by it.

We were in class when Mr. Moore stepped out to Xerox some papers. Of course we all took total advantage of the unmonitored moment and started throwing paper and chalk at one another.

We were having a ball. Spitballs, paper balls, chalk and erasers were flying all around the room. During the midst of playing for some unknown reason this one kid named Charles McKale stood on top of his desk and took the liberty of saying to the prettiest girl in the class, "You black Bitch."

It was almost as if all of our spit balls and everything else stopped in mid air and hit the ground. All of the games suddenly stopped and everyone looked at him astonished, even the white kids. Then out of nowhere this Spanish girl stood up on her desk pointing at me and yelled, "Giovanni, after school you better kick his ass!" Before I knew it the entire class started chanting, "kick his ass, kick his ass, kick his ass! I thought to myself, "Out of everyone in our class why did she have to volunteer me?"

If These Streets Could Talk

Although everyone thought I was so cool because I was from Philly, I was a little leery because Charles had three or four older brothers who were notorious for jumping people. Plus, Charles had a 7-0 schoolyard fight record and I didn't want to be number eight on his list, but to no avail I had to fight. Peer pressure is something else.

At 3:00 pm when the dismissal bell rang, everyone headed toward the infamous train tracks which was the unauthorized after school fight zone. Charles and I walked side-by-side ready for combat with a parade of shouting and yelling kids following closely behind us. I was trying to psych myself up for the fight thinking about something that really made me mad because deep down inside I wasn't even angry enough to fight Charles, but like I said, in 6th grade peer pressure is at its peak.

Although I did admire Charles for having the heart to stand up for his honor, this was one fight that I could not lose. My reputation was on the line in two ways. One, not only would a win make Vanessa Daniels my girlfriend, but it would also confirm that Philly people are not to be messed with. Besides, there's nothing worse than getting beat up in front of the entire school.

Once we reached the train tracks we faced each other as the crowd formed a human boxing ring around us. When I looked at the crowd around us not only was my entire 6th grade class present to witness this brawl but it looked as if half of the school was there. My heart was pounding so hard on my chest when I looked down I seen my tee shirt moving. Charles stepped right up in my face.

"What are you going to do little nigger Philly boy?"

That's was all that I needed to hear.

"Crack."

If These Streets Could Talk

I threw the best overhand right that I had ever thrown in my life right across his jaw. I followed up with a flurry of lefts and rights not giving him a chance to retaliate.

Case always taught me that the best fight is the one where you don't get hit.

When Charles went down I immediately started kicking and stomping him. Then all of a sudden I noticed that he was not moving. The crowd's yells and cheers turned silent and a look of concern ran across everyone's faces. You see rumor had it that Charles had a metal plate in his head from a childhood bicycle accident. They say that's why he was a little crazy.

A few people took off running afraid of him being dead and not wanting anything to do with it. My heart was pounding even faster, but I had to stand my ground because like I said, my reputation was on the line.

When I looked down at Charles I noticed his chest moving up and down indicating that he was breathing.

"You ain't dead motherfucker!"

I kicked him right in his mouth. Charles jumped up screaming holding his mouth, face dirty, mouth bleeding, and ran away crying like a baby.

"You better watch your back boy. This ain't over," he threatened.

The remainder of the crowd started yelling my name and lifted me up in the air like I just kicked the winning field goal in the Super Bowl. Charles was a known troublemaker who always picked on the younger kids and was overdue for a butt whipping, and I gave it to him.

Needless to say my reputation elevated to a new high.

If These Streets Could Talk

After the Charles incident me and this kid named Allen, who was the school bully, became really close because we had several things in common. We both were good at sports, we both smoked weed, and we both loved the girls. Although I was only 13 years old I have to admit I had a strong attraction to girls. My hormones were going haywire. Me and Allen used to sneak girls down to his basement after school, since his father was a single parent and always worked late, and convince them to make out with us for candy. I even took Allen to 7-11 and taught him how to steal candy bars and hoagies and sell them in the playground before and after school.

Living with a kleptomaniac taught me how to steal rather well or at least I thought.

Me and Allen were in 7-11 on our usual stealing detail. When we walked in the store, he would go one way and I would go the other.

The manager was behind the counter making coffee and there were no other customers in the store at the time. Me and Allen gave each other the eye from a distant indicating that our mission was accomplished so it was time to leave the store. As we were getting ready to exit, the manager jumped from over the counter and grabbed both of us by our jackets.

"I got you too little asses now!"

Allen snatched away from his grip and ran out of the door leaving me tussling with the manager.

"Get off of me!" I cried as I to tried to snatch away from the store manager's grip.

I tried to fight him but he was too big and strong. He then drug me over to the potato chip rack. The whole time I was kicking and cursing he pulled some hand cuffs out of his back pocket and cuffed me to the rack. Then he went over to the phone and called the police.

If These Streets Could Talk

The cops were pretty cool. When they put me in their car they just drove me to my godmother's house and let me go. She darn near fainted at the thought of me stealing but deep down inside I think she knew my godfather influenced my behavior. My godmother sat me down in the living room.

"Giovonni you know I love you with all of my heart. I opened up my home to you and give you everything that a child could want. I knew from the beginning you didn't want to be here but me and KK want to give you a better environment to grow up in but you still insist on doing wrong. What is the problem?"

I looked up at her.

"I miss my family."

She just gave me a warm smile and rubbed her hand across the side of my face. "I knew that was it. I just tried to show you something else but there is nothing like family." She just walked into the kitchen, picked up the phone, and called KK.

While they were talking I went upstairs and started packing my things. I loved my godmother, but she was a little too old and sick to take care of an out of control teenager. Plus there's no stronger love than the love of your family. Although my family was totally dysfunctional, they were all I had and all I knew.

The next morning my godmother walked me to the bus stop with Cuddles. Her eyes were watery the whole time, and I tried not to look at her. When we got to the bus stop we sat on the bench. She put her hand on my knee.

"Giovonni I want you to remember something. This is a cruel world that we live in. It will beat you down to the ground and take everything from your soul, but only if you let it. That's why you have to make your own decisions and deal with adversity as it comes. Nobody is going to give you anything for free. You have to earn everything you get especially you being a man, and don't ever let anyone take your dreams or tell you that you can't do something. You can be anything you want to in life with hard work, dedication, and determination. Now, I've tried to show you a different side of life because it's important to be diverse, so take what you've learned from living over here in NJ and store it in your mind forever. Now you go out there and be a good strong man"

She handed me an envelope. I assumed it had money in it.

"Here's a little pocket change. If you ever need me for anything at all you call me. You know you're always welcome back."

She coughed a few times while holding her chest then caught her breath and gave me a big hug and kiss. I bent down and hugged Cuddles.

"You protect my mom while I'm gone you hear me boy?"

He wagged his tail and whimpered as if he knew he wasn't going to see me anymore, and he was right. That following year my Godmother's heart gave out on her, and she died. I think I was the only thing that kept her going, and when I left so did she. The last I heard my Godfather sold the house and got rid of Cuttles. What a looser.

It felt so good to be back on the "W". Since I got sent back to Philly in the middle of the school year I had to attend Sayre Jr. High school, which was a lot tougher than Mequan or any NJ school. Although a lot of my neighborhood friends went there, I was still considered one of the new kids, so I received new kid treatment.

Once I stopped at my locker while changing classes, and the halls were full of students. My next class was gym, so I put my watch and money in my locker. Out of nowhere I heard my name called loudly, "Giovonni!" Like I said, the halls were full of students going to class so I tried to look through the crowd to see who had called me. After a few seconds of not recognizing anyone, I turned around to lock my locker and just like that my watch and money were gone as everyone walked past me like nothing had happened. That was my first time ever being played and there was nothing I could do about it, but it made me sharper. I never got played like that again.

I had a friend named Arthur Jenkins who I got pretty tight with. He and his mom came to Philly from Florida, so he was a little country to me. Like myself, he too enjoyed the ever so wonderful intoxicating feeling of smoking marijuana so our common interest made it natural for us to bond.

Art and I wouldn't only get high off of weed. We would occasionally smoke opium and sometime snort record cleaner or "Rush," as they called it. It was a early form of huffing.

My boy Art was a very mischievous and adventurous person with a unique sense of humor. Example: once on our way to school, the two of us had walked past some guy working under the hood of his truck. We had just smoked some weed and both of us noticed the crack of his ass showing from the back of his jeans. Art was drinking a soda.

"Yo G, get a head start running because I'm gonna bust this dude in his ass with this bottle. I tried to plead with him not to do it because I was too high to run, but I started laughing at the thought of it.

"Art, man don't do it, "I said as I started slowly jogging away still cracking up knowing when Art said he was going to do something, he was going to do it. Art crept up behind the working man. "Crack!" The man hit his head on the hood of the truck and let out a howling cry. When he jumped from off of the bumper of the truck he pulled out a twelve inch Rambo knife. "I'm going to kill you two little bastards!"

If These Streets Could Talk

Me and Art took off running towards our school. Art grabbed me by my wrist pulling me to run faster. "Run G, run!"

When we reached the front door of our school I thought we were safe except the knife yielding man ran into the school right behind us still yelling, "I'm going to kill yaw when I catch yaw."

I couldn't believe this guy was still chasing us. The halls were empty since classes had already started so this maniac was on the loose.

We ran up the fire escape steps, through the gym, then into the hallway leading back to the fire escape finally loosing Mr. Butt Crack. We both sat on the steps totally out of breath shaking scared. "I told you not to hit that dude with that bottle." Art looked at me and we both burst out laughing then went to class.

There weren't many white people that went to our school but there was this beautiful white girl who attended Sayre Jr. High School named Heather. She claimed that her dad was black but we never saw him and her characteristics didn't have a trace of him in her. She had naturally curly blonde hair and blue-green eyes that were mesmerizing to look at: almost like staring into the ocean. And since she grew up in the hood, she talked with a black girl twist of not enunciating her words and talking a lot of slang. She was in the 9th grade and me and Art were in the 7th grade. Since Heather was a few years older than us she also had a after school job at Gino's down Center City. Those of you who don't know KFC used to be called Gino's back in the day. (Look it up if you don't believe).

We would meet her after work and smoke weed with her when she got off, and of course she supplied the chicken for our munchies.

This one afternoon Heather had some weed that she insisted that we try.

" I stole this from my big brother and it's some serious shit!" she stated while rolling the joint.

"Well then light it up," Art insisted passing her his lighter.

As we were smoking I started to feel really weird. Not like I would normally feel from smoking a joint. I felt extremely high.

While the two of them were laughing and talking, their voices started to echo. I shook my head from side to side trying to shake away the echo but it wouldn't leave. I turned to Heather.

"What kind of weed is this?"

She casually responded, "Oh it's just dust... dust... dust....dust..?"

I instantly got paranoid. I couldn't believe this girl had just slipped me some angel dust and acted like it wasn't a big deal.

"What do you mean dust ...dust ...dust....:"

I started hyperventilating.

"Oh shit... shit.... shit....shit" I said holding my chest trying to catch my breath.

Then all of a sudden everything started moving in slow motion. I was discombobulated. I felt like I had to get home immediately. I stood up and started walking.

"Where are you going G?" Heather asked looking concerned as I walked away from her and Art.

"Man fuck yaw. I got to get out of here...here...here...here." I said as I felt like I just floated away. I heard the two of them laughing in the background as I just drifted away.

As I headed to the train I decided to stop at the news stand and buy some potato chips and a snickers bar with my train fare. There's something about that sugar and salt mixture that is so satisfying when you have the munchies.

Behind the train platform there was a set of bars with a gap big enough for a small person like myself to squeeze through and get onto the El without paying. When I got down to the bottom of the steps where me and Art would normally sneak onto the train, I felt like someone was looking so I was scared to squeeze between the bars thinking I was going to get caught. The strange thing was that there was no one around to see me but in my mind, I was being watched.

After about thirty minutes of paranoia, I slid through the bars and got onto the train.

On the train I was as nervous as a hostage. It was the 5:00 clock rush hour and the train was full of passengers. I felt like everyone on the train was watching me. I just stood up and held onto the pole looking straight ahead, eyes as big as light bulbs, wishing everyone would just stop looking at me.

After the dust incident, I never smoked another joint that I didn't personally role myself. I enjoyed getting high but I didn't get off on hallucinating. Give me some regular weed any day.

If These Streets Could Talk

Ch 5 School Is Not Cool

In high school weed became a part of me. Whenever I wanted to feel good or just zone out, I would buy a bag. Eventually Case taught me how to sell it. Back in 1980, you could get ten to fifteen joints out of a $5 bag so I would sell $1 joints in the boy's bathroom between classes. It seemed as if everyone was smoking weed. Eventually the money started flowing so abundantly that I started putting my boy Jones down with my hustle.

My boy Anthony Jones was my life long best friend and also a popular athlete at BOK Vocational Technical High School. Our motto at BOK was, "you had to Be Ok to go to BOK. Get it B- Ok, BOK? Anyway, his mom and pop were very strict plus they were deeply into church. I actually felt sorry for Jones because he would have to go to church for everything. Bible study, choir practice, usher meetings, church picnics, church banquets, bake sales, fundraisers, or anything else that had to do with church. He stayed at church so much I don't know how he had time to play sports, but he did and he was good. He had God given talent. The boy was very strong and could run so fast that if he got past you, there was no catching up.

Since I knew Jones was popular being a jock and all, my plan was to get the football team, basketball team, and all his little girlfriends on my weed payroll, and slowly but surely it worked. You see, Case was my supply man and whenever he got a large supply of killer gold weed or tystick (a rare type of marijuana) I would give Jones a couple of free samples to give out to his teammates and friends.

Before I knew it, half of the school was hooked. Jones started selling so much weed for me that he started smoking himself just to see what all the hype was about. We were making $10 profit off of every $5 bag of joints that we bought and the turnover was nonstop.

If These Streets Could Talk

By the middle of the school year, everything was going smooth until one day after third period in the boy's bathroom we were counting our money and three guys from South Philly came in. One was short, about my height, and the other two were jocks like Jones. The shortest one stepped right up in my face.

"We're tired of yaw West Philly niggas coming down our neighborhood making all this money in our territory, so give it the fuck up!" Then he shoved both hands into my chest.

I didn't like to fight but Case always taught me not to let anybody take anything from you because you'll be marked on the streets as a chump.

I stepped up a little closer to him and sucker kicked him so hard in his balls that we both fell to the ground.

When he balled up on the floor in a fetal position I thought I killed him because I never heard a human being make a noise like the one I heard coming from his mouth. Jones immediately rushed one of his compadres while the biggest one grabbed me and threw me into one of the bathroom stalls.

While Jones and the other dude were tussling around on the ground, Andre the Giant had his hands around the back of my neck and was trying to put my face in the toilet bowl.

"Yeah West Philly. We're going swimming today," he said while trying to put my head in the toilet.

Although he was three times my size, I was not going to let this guy put my head in the toilet. I was trying to punch and elbow him with all of my strength but my candy bar punches didn't affect him at all.

While he was still trying to push my head down in the bowl, I had my hands on the toilet seat and with all of my strength I stretched my legs out to where I was in a sort of push up position with my hands gripped on the edge of the bowl not allowing my face to go into the water. I knew if my face hit that water I would have been totally humiliated throughout the entire school . If you got baptized in a toilet bowl, all of your cool points go straight out of the window.

Then all of a sudden I heard a loud familiar adult voice.

"What in the hell is going on in here?"

It was Mr. Nelson our Chemistry teacher. Gigantor took the death grip off of me and I fell on the floor. My arms were weak and felt like spaghetti, and I was totally exhausted but still dry. Then Gigantor ran over to Mr. Nelson.

"Mr. Nelson, these two boys stole the money my mom gave me to pay her electric bill after school," with a totally innocent look. Mr. Nelson snatched me from off of the floor and violently searched my pockets confiscating my $325.

" Everybody to the principle's office right now!"

We all marched single file with Mr. Nelson walking closely behind us.

Mr. Fisher our principal didn't like me and I didn't like him. The reason was my oldest sister Rochelle cursed our family's last name at the school when she threw hot coffee in his face for trying to touch her butt one day after cheerleader practice. Of course he denied it, but since it was her word against his he remained the principal and every chance he got he tried to dog one of us Pizarros.

Without even hearing my side of the story Mr. Fisher immediately gave my money to Godzilla and suspended me and Jones for five days each. Jones damn near fainted from the verdict because he knew the butt whipping his dad was going to put on him when he got home. I was so used to getting beatings that I didn't even care about the suspension. I just wanted my money back.

Jones whined and complained all the way home on the bus.

"My pops is going to kill me when I tell him that I'm suspended. I can't believe I let you talk me into selling weed. I **knew** God would punish me for this."

He actually started crying and praying on the bus. He was really pissing me off.

I mentally blocked him out. All I could think about was my $325 that big bird had of mine. My head boiled over with anger. All I could see was red. Revenge was a must.

That evening at home I convinced myself that I had to slay a giant.

I bought a six inch piece of lead pipe from the hardware store and wrapped duct tape around one end of it to make a sure grip. I hit it against the palm of my hand a few times to test the security of the grip. Case taught me to never loose your weapon or get disarmed in a battle because it could cost you your life. I looked at myself in the mirror as I hit the pipe against my hand. Talking to myself while looking in the mirror.

"He thinks it's sweet taking my money like that. I got something for his ass tomorrow."

My home girl Winny from 56th street also went to BOK. She was beautiful and sexy, and I told her what happened in the boys room and that I needed her help.

"Ok, pretend like you want to go out with Goliath and have him walk you to the subway after school."

"All right but what's in it for me," holding her hand out. I handed her a nickel bag of weed. She smiled that pretty smile and slid it into her bra.

"Consider it done."

After school the following day I snuck into the teachers' parking lot to Mr. Nelson's and Mr. Fisher's car. I pulled my ice pick out of my book bag and flattened all of their tires. Then I made my way to the subway.

From a distance I could see Winny and Goliath walking my way. Seeing him in daylight walking next to Winny allowed me to see how big he really was. I figured he was about 6'1' 220 pounds. I was only 5'5 and 145 lb. soaking wet so my pipe was a necessary instrument of destruction.

He was looking real goofy carrying Winny's book bag down the street. I also noticed he was wearing a brand new pair of shell top Adidas sneakers.

"No he didn't buy no shells with my cash," I thought making me even angrier.

I ducked behind a building as they both walked past me then I followed them creeping a few feet behind them. As they approached the top of the subway stairs I eased up behind him sliding my homemade assault weapon out of the front of my pants.

"Yo homie."
He started to turn around.

I stood behind him with my pipe raised high in the air. As he turned around "*crack.*" I hit him right in the middle of his for head with everything I had. His head open right up like a melon and blood instantly started flowing out. He fell to the ground flat on his back and was unconscious. I heard screams as a few on- lookers watched in disbelief as I was searching through his pockets while he was out cold.

"Where's my money motherfucker!" I said while standing over him ripping his pockets off of his jeans.

Whinny was fake screaming and crying to make it look good as she ran away.

All he had left of my money was $63 so I took that, snatched his sneakers off his feet ,although they were twice my size, put them in my book bag, and gave him a hard kick to the ribs. I could hear the train coming, so I ran down the subway steps, jumped on the train and headed home.

When I got home I went straight to Rochelle's apartment and told Case what had just taken place.

"That's what he gets," was Case's response." If you would've done anything less I would be whippin your ass right now. He got just what he deserved. Two wrongs don't make a right but it damn sure makes it even."

It made me feel good knowing that Case condoned my behavior so I gave him the sneakers. They were just his size.

The following day at BOK, Jones met me at our normal meeting place, a small Italian deli called Esposito's in South Philly. They made the best hoagies in the city. I swear the meat there is so fresh you would think they were killing and cutting the animals in the back of the store.

As soon as Jones saw me he pulled me outside the store.

"Yo man, that nigga Craig is in the hospital with about 35 stitches in his head," You really split his wig G."

"I don't know Jones. I just lost it when I seen him sporting some new sneakers with my money."

"Yeah but now we got to watch our backs. You know these South Philly cats are slimy. They might try to come back with the come back."

Jones started to walk away then turned back to look at me.

"Follow me so I can show you something"

Inside school Jones took me to a locker that the two of us shared.

"Look inside."

I peeked in a saw what appeared to be a sawed off shotgun.

"Man where in the hell did you get that from?"

"Don't worry about that, I got my connects."

I took a hard look at Jones. It was 8:15am, school hadn't started yet and his eyes were bloodshot red. I knew it was from the marijuana effect. He was wearing a new TI sweat suit with a matching Kangol and a thick gold chain. He also had on a brand new pair of shell top Adidas. I thought to myself, "Damn I'm really corrupting Jones."

At lunch time I was in line getting my food when Jones rushed over to me.

"Dude, what ever you do don't sit with me at lunch today."

Then he rushed away. I thought he was still hallucinating from the early morning marijuana so I got my lunch and started to head over towards him to find out what he was babbling about.

As I approached him a hand grabbed my shoulder.

"Come with us."

It was Mr. Fisher, a school security guard, and a Philadelphia Police Officer. They all escorted me to my locker.

Class was about to start so the hallways were full of students and everyone was whispering, looking, and pointing at me. When we got to my locker Mr. Fisher grabbed me by the back of my shirt.

"Open it!"

At first I tried to act like I forgot the combination until he smacked me in the back of my head.

"I said open it!"

I gave him a mean look as I unlocked the lock and opened the locker.

"Pull it out!"

"Pull what out?"

I tried to look confused. He gripped me by my collar this time slamming me against the locker really hard.

"Don't play with me boy."

I reached in and pulled out the shotgun.

Well, before I knew it the Philly cop pulled out his revolver and pointed it to my head.

"Drop it right now!"

I carefully laid the gun down and the fake school cop slammed me against the locker almost breaking my nose then hand-cuffed me.

"Man that ain't mine. I don't know how it got there."

"Save it for David. We got your little ass now, and I know you were the one who flattened my tires you little bastard."

When we got to Mr. Fisher's office, I was surprised to see Jones already there with another police officer. He had already made a full confession that the gun was his and for some reason he even said he was the one who slashed Mr. Fisher's tires. I thought to myself, "Jones could have pinned everything on me, but instead he took the rap. Now that's what I call loyalty."

Well, it turned out that the sawed off shot-gun of Jones was just a BB gun. Mr. Fisher was furious.

"Take your little ass back to class and you better believe I'll be watching you," he yelled at me as I walked out of his office.

I pretended to go back to class and left out of a side door of the building never returning to BOK Vocational Technical School again. Jones on the other hand got his usual tongue thrashing and butt lashing from his dad. I really admired Jones for taking the rap because I can't say that I would have done the same for him, but after that our bond became even tighter.

When I told KK what had happened the very next day she transferred me to West Philadelphia High, which was an even bigger mistake since all of my neighborhood friends went there. All I did was cut class, smoke weed, and go to the movies.

If These Streets Could Talk

I was only sixteen years old and started really dropping behind in school. I got left down two years in a row. Not for academic failure but for attendance. The sad thing about it was when I did attend class I was an A & B student. My mathematic skills were excellent, I could read and comprehend very well, but I had a problem retaining the information that I had read. (Probably from all of the marijuana that I smoked.) They say it kills your short-term memory and I was living proof so my teacher thought it best that I attend summer school.

KK found this small private school in Center City called Delaware Valley High. It had accelerated classes for people like myself who had fallen behind in school two or more years and wanted to catch up. Every day around lunch time Jones would meet with me downtown at summer school and we would go behind the school parking lot and smoke a joint and eat some snacks. I would then go back to class in la la land making the class work more fascinating than it really was.

One thing about marijuana, it brings out the philosopher in you. I mean you can take a simple subject and totally run away with it.

On one of our usual weed smoking occasions me and Jones were lying on top of some parked cars behind my school looking up in the sky.

"Here G, light this up."

Before I lit it I smelled it through the paper making sure that it was just marijuana. Although I trusted Jones I never wanted to experience the dust incident again.

"Dam Jones, what kind of weed is this?"

"Oh, that's some of that stuff that they are trying to keep out of the country but that small amount made it through."

"Yeah whatever."

I smiled and lit it up.

I noticed the taste was very unique like some weed that I had never tasted before. The buzz came on almost immediately. Then came the philosophy.

"Yo G man."

"That's my name."

"Do you realize that the nickel is the most least respected of all United States currency?"

I looked over at Jones in disbelief.

"Man I knew it was something in this weed,."

"No man seriously, think about it. A penny ain't worth shit but it only takes five of them to equal a nickel. Plus the nickel is bigger and thicker than a dime but has less value. The nickel gets no respect," he said as I passed him back the joint.

I immediately joined in.

"Oh, now I see where you're coming from. All right, dig this. All of the other silver coins have ridges on the sides of them but Mr. Nickel is just smoothed out on the sides and shit. Plus, on the dime President Roosevelt got a fresh haircut. Why does Washington have to be wearing a ponytail? Man that's fucked up."

We looked at each other and burst into a hysterical laughter.

For the rest of the afternoon Jones hung around Center City at the arcade waiting for me to get out of class. When my last class was over he met me outside. We lit up a joint as we walked to catch the El back to West Philly.

We got off the train at 56th St.

"Hold up for a second. I want to get some munchies."

Jones walked into the corner store while I stayed outside.

"Hurry up man, it's hot as fish grease out here."

It was 3:00pm mid July and the sun was beaming down so hard you could see the heat-rays coming from off of the tar in the street.

If These Streets Could Talk

We both were wearing our Gazels (designer sunglasses) and bucket hats to protect us from the sun. When Jones came out of the store all I remember him saying was,

"Let's cross over to the shady side of the street."

"Crack!"

Out of nowhere something hit me in my right ear so hard that my sunglasses, hat, and book bag all flew off simultaneously. I stumbled a few feet and fell so hard into a parked car that my head print was indented into the passenger side door. I thought that a car had just hit me. I was dazed but still conscious.

As my vision became clearer I was able to focus on the object coming towards me. As my focus became clearer I saw that it was Craig, the dude's head that I had busted.

"Get the fuck up faggot and take this ass whippin like a man!"

I saw two more of his boys across the street trying to get past the oncoming traffic to cross over to the other side to get me. That's when I shook off my semi-conscious state and took off running.

Everything happened so fast. Craig grabbed the back of my shirt but I tore away leaving him with a piece of my Izoid shirt in his right hand from the Barry Sanders back spin I put on him. I then shook his boys and at the same time avoided getting hit by another moving car.

As the G bus that runs down 56th St. was loading and unloading passengers on the corner, people looked startled as I ran past moving cars ducking punches as Craig and his hit squad tried to ambush me.

As all of this was going on it gradually dawned on me where is Jones? Did he set me up? Did he run out on me? Why the hell isn't he running too?

If These Streets Could Talk

The next thing I heard was…

"Move G move!" POW, POW POW. "Move!"

I looked across the street and Jones was running towards me shooting at Craig and his boys. People at the bus stop started screaming and running into stores and ducking behind parked cars for shelter. The bus that was loading passengers on and off the bus closed the doors and peeled off.

"Kill them motherfuckers!" I yelled as I ducked too from Jones uncontrolled gun fire.

At that moment Jones was my hero because I knew those big dudes would have killed me. Craig and his boys scattered like cock roaches in the kitchen when you turn on the lights at 3:00 am to get a glass of water.

Me and Jones heard police sirens from a distance so we ran towards the "W" which was only two blocks away.

We both ran straight to the first floor and told Case what had happened. I couldn't believe he actually thought it was funny.

"Well bighead you got your first experience of retaliation," He said while laughing. "You put your guard down after you cracked that boy's head and that was a major mistake. You thought that it was over since some time had passed. Well guess what? 'It ain't over until it's over. Unless you kill a nigga or beat his ass real bad, you have to constantly watch your back for the sneak attack."

Case grabbed me by my chin and spun my face around towards him to examine my ear.

"Man look at your ear. It looks like he hit you with a brick," he said still laughing.

As my adrenalin level lowered, my pain level increased. My ear was really pounding with pain. The way my ear looked he must have been wearing a ring or something I thought.

I went over to the mirror and seen my right ear was twice the size as my left and was bleeding. My first thought was retaliation but then I thought to myself that if someone had busted my head the way I did Craig's, I would have reacted the same way.

Jones asked, "So what do you want to do, go down South Philly on a seek and destroy mission?"

I looked again in the mirror and thought for a second.

"Naw man, lets let it ride for now."

Then something else dawned on me.

"And by the way Jones, where in the hell did you get a real gun from?"

If These Streets Could Talk

Ch 6 Joy Rides

Beep Beep. "Jump in."

It was Shank driving a brand new 1981 Nissan Z28.

"Yo Shank, where did you get **this** from?" I was amazed. It was the first time I had seen one up close and personal.

"Where in the hell do you think I got it from?" He plucked his cigarette from the opening of the T-top.

Oh, by the way, Shank was a thief. In fact he lived in a household of thieves. His whole family did everything from stealing and robbing to credit card scams and identity theft. At sixteen, his older brothers had taught him how to hot-wire cars, file the serial numbers down, and sell the cars on the streets or to the chop shop. Shank was a pretty cool guy but real shady. You could never put your guard down around him because he'd get you. It was in his bloodline.

I also hated his buckteeth. He was in real bad need of braces. His teeth had so many gaps between them that they looked like piano keys.

"Man this thing is real nice," I said as I excitedly jumped in.

"Yea, it is ain't it?"

It had a T-top, AM/FM cassette, tan leather interior and a mega BOSE system.

I immediately jumped in and we started cruzin through the neighborhood catchin all eyes.

I saw a couple of cuties walking by.

"Hey Shorty, can I get your phone number?" I yelled out of the car.

"Not from the passenger side you can't."

They just giggled at me and kept walking.

"Man chill out and stop yellin those corny ass lines out of my window. This here is a girl magnet. Just sit back, relax, and watch how they cling."

After hearing that I rolled a fat joint and laid back in my seat relaxed.

Shank was right. At every stop light girls were smiling and winking at us. A few of them even gave us their phone numbers without us even asking.

This was right up my alley. I didn't know all it took was a nice car to pull women. I was hyped up.

"Yo man, you got's to let me sport these wheels tonight!" I insisted.

"Yo man, you got's to let me get some of that killer weed," pointing to my joint.

"No problemo Amigo. For these wheels I'll hook you up something real nice."

Later that afternoon I met shank on the "W" with an ounce of weed in a clear sandwich bag. We exchanged keys for weed.

"Be careful G," he warned me.

I got in the driver's seat.

"This baby got some kick to it. Plus my brother wants to use it tomorrow night to take his girl out."

"Man you don't have nothing to worry about. I can wheelie a Mack Truck. I'll return your keys tomorrow same time, same place."

We shook hands and he opened the sandwich bag and sniffed the contents.

"Now that's what I'm talkin about. A gift from the earth."

He put the sandwich bag in his front pocket and walked away smiling.

If These Streets Could Talk

Now I don't know why I was faking it because my driving skills were not up to par. Case had me behind the wheel a few times but he said his heart couldn't take it.

I sat in the parked car for a few minutes examining all of the gadgets on the dash board to familiarize myself with the vehicle. I smoked a joint to relax until I was ready to drive off.

Shank was right. That Z28 had so much power that when I pulled out of the parking space I almost hit three people who were crossing the street. I drove around the neighborhood for a while and once I got the feel of the power I was ready to show off in my stolen rented vehicle

My first stop was 52nd Street in West Philly. This is the place, better known as the Strip, was a place that you could buy anything from clothing to jewelry to drugs to guns or women. You could also get stuck up or your pocketbook snatched if you weren't careful.

I seen my homegirl Sweets standing on the corner with some of our friends. She got that name because every time you see her she would be eating some candy or gum or something sweet. She was only fourteen years old but acted twenty-four, very fast for her age. She always hung around the older crowd trying to be down with the streets.

Beep! Beep! When Sweets turned around her eyes lit up.

"Oh my god G, you came up!" She ran towards my car.

Rubbing my chin, "Yeah well you know, it's just a little somethin, somethin."

She didn't even open the door. She jumped right in the opening of the T-top.

"I'm telling you right now; throw that damn gum away before you even think about sittin on these butter leather seats."

"Aw shut up and start driving," she said while tossing the gum out of the window.

If These Streets Could Talk

Sweets loved the fast life. Fast money, fast guys, and fast cars. She would always be in somebody's car or on the back of someone's motorcycle. I always thought she was a little cutie but never pursued her. She was a little too fast for me. I kind of looked at her as a little sister.

While driving down 52nd street we made a right onto Market St. While we were cruising down the street we would stop at almost every corner to talk to people we knew. All of our friends were waving and saying how fly we looked in that Z28. We felt like two movie stars.

I passed Sweets my sandwich bag and she rolled a joint, laid her head back, and put on her sunglasses while her thick, black, wavy hair blew in the wind.

"G, you're one smooth dude."

"Sweets baby, you **never** lie."

We both laughed while at the same time coughing from the weed.

After we finished smoking our joint we rode around for a while jamming to a Sugar Hill Gang tape that Shank had in the cassette deck. As we approached the stoplight I looked in my rear view mirror and noticed a police wagon slowly pulling up behind us.

"Ow snap, 5-0."

I sat up in my seat and put both of my hands on the steering wheel ten O'clock and two O'clock.

"Where?"

Sweets was getting ready to turn around to look behind us.

"Sit up straight!"

I grabbed her arm and spun her back around in her seat.

I was trying to look normal and drive slow but the wagon followed my every move. I made a left, they made a left. At the very next traffic light they flashed their blue and red lights indicating me to pull over. I thought to myself, "I don't have no license, registration, or insurance plus the car is stolen. I'm not going to jail."

I slammed my foot on the gas pedal and peeled off. Me and Sweets heads slammed back into the headrests of the seats from the burst of acceleration.

"What the hell are you doing G?

"Hold on Sweets!"

I concentrated on trying to keep the vehicle steady as I peeled down the street.

That Z28 went from 0 to 60 in less than five seconds. My heart was racing and my high disappeared. It was on. I got an instant adrenalin rush as the vehicles RPM gauge shot into the red zone.

I looked out of my rear-view mirror and seen that I had about a one block lead on the slow patty wagon. Sweets was yelling and hitting my arm begging me to stop

"G you got to stop. You're going to get us killed!"

I just blocked her out trying to focus on the road.

I looked again out of my rear view mirror watching, as the police wagon got smaller in the mirror as the gap between us got larger.

When I looked in front of me, out of the blue, I saw what appeared to be drunken Joe staggering across the street. I had to do something quick because I only had two options: One I could hit and most likely kill Joe or two I could hit the steel beam that supported the Market Street El and maybe kill me and Sweets.

"Crash!"

All I seen was a flash of light.

The Z28 literally rapped around the iron support beam. With a bunch of dust and smoke filling the air, I felt extremely light headed but I was able to open the door and stagger out of the mangled wreck. I looked back at the car and saw Sweets lying on what was left of the hood of the car with blood and broken glass on her face and in her hair.

"Come on Sweets we got to go," shrugging on her shoulder. She was unconscious.

I was in my semi conscious state as I shook her shoulder once more but she wasn't moving. I felt real weak at the knees and my vision was blurry as if I were going to faint but I composed myself enough to run away.

I looked up at the street sign and realized that I was on 48th street near the high-rise apartment complexes, AKA The Projects so I headed towards the projects as I heard the sirens getting nearer.

When I reached the projects I ran all the way up to the 11th floor stumbling over bums and junkies asleep in the steps all the way up to my boy Larry's apartment 1102. Larry's mom's apartment was the known gambling spot. Every weekend his mother would have card and crap games. The problem was if you would win you would have to figure out how to get out of the projects with your winnings without being robbed. When ever I won I would have Case and Tommy come pick me up.

When Larry's mom answered the door I tried to look normal but it felt like my wrist was broken and I was out of breath.

With a fake smile I composed myself.
"Hi Mrs. Davis, is Larry home?"
Looking at me strangely, she asked

"What in the hell is wrong with you boy?"

"Nothing M'am, the elevator is broken."

"Oh yeah, what else is new?"

As she opened the door the mixed smell of chitterlings cooking and cigarette and cigar smoke almost made me vomit.

I looked around the room and saw a couple of older guys were sitting around a table playing cards and drinking moonshine.

"Larry, G is here to see you!" She yelled to the back of the apartment.

" Then send him the hell back," he responded to his mother.

Larry was a friend of mine from Sayre Jr. High School. We became tight after I helped him when these two guys were trying to jump him. I didn't even know him. I just jumped in the fight and we were cool ever since.

I also knew a deep dark secret about Larry.

You see once I spent the night over Larry's house and his mother called him into her bedroom. It was around 1:00 am and all of her company had went home. I don't think she knew I was still there. She was drunk that night and when he went into her room he didn't come back for awhile but I had to go to the bathroom. As I headed to the bathroom I walked past her bedroom and what I saw next was unbelievable. I peeked in a little closer and saw her make him take down his pants and climb on top of her. I couldn't believe my eyes. She was molesting him. Her own son. It was one of the most disturbing things that I had ever witnessed in my entire life. I later found out she had been doing it for years or at least since Larry's father died when he was eight years old.

When Larry came back to bed I think he heard me going to the bathroom and knew that I saw what had happened. All he said was, "I hate it here," and then he got in bed. I guess that's why Larry talks to his mom with no respect.

In Larry's bedroom I told him everything that had just taken place earlier that evening.

"Wait a minute. So you're telling me that Sweets is dead?"

I was sitting on his bed rocking back and forth visualizing the entire incident.

"I don't know man, I don't know"

"How in the hell are you gonna just leave Sweets on top of a car like that?"

"I was scared Ok! I just couldn't stop running."

He walked out of his room.

"Were are you goin man," I said fearfully.

He came back into the room a few minutes later and threw me a bag of ice for my wrist.

"You better chill out here tonight and we'll see what's up in the morning. Take the top bunk and if I hear any snoring, your ass is outta here."

"Thanks man," I said as I climbed gingerly into the top of his bunk bed.

As the two of us laid in the dark I could feel that both of us had a lot on our mind.

"Hey G, you up?"

"Yea man what's up?"

"I need you to promise me something."

"Anything man."

Promise me that you won't tell anyone about my moms. She been through a lot since my pops died and I don't want nothing to happen to her. I'm all she's got."

I started to explain to him how wrong it was what his mom was doing to him how she needed help and what she was doing to him was not the cure. It was sick. But then I though how devastating it must be being victimized by your own mother.

"Don't worry man. As far as I'm concerned it never happened."

If These Streets Could Talk

"Thanks man." He dozed off to sleep.

That night I couldn't sleep at all. All that I could think about was Sweet's young motionless body lying on the hood of that car. I started thinking about leaving the city if she was dead or if she was alive would she lead the police to my house. I had all kinds of bad thoughts and nightmares that night.

The next morning Larry cooked up breakfast and made a few phone calls to some of our friends. He found out that Sweets was alive and she was at Misericordia Hospital in stable condition. He also found out that she had told the police that she didn't know the driver of the stolen car. She told them that she was waiting for the bus and he offered her a ride so she took it Larry said Sweets gave the police a totally opposite description of me the driver. He was 6'2", very light skinned, with a Kid & Play boxed haircut. I figured that story should keep them busy for awhile.

Larry gave me a change of clothes, which were about twice my size.

"Thanks man, I'll return your stuff tomorrow."

"Man you can keep that shit. That's old gear. You just ought to be thankful that Sweets ain't dead or no snitch."

"Yea I know. I owe her big time".

We shook hands, hugged, and then I left.

When I left the projects I walked straight down Market Street. There, on 48th and Market was the Z28 still wrapped around the steel beam with yellow police tape around it. I seen drops of Sweets blood on the hood of the car and a chill ran down my spine recalling how she looked flying through that windshield.

I stopped at the flower stand on 52nd and Market Street and bought one dozen of roses. Then I walked down to the deli and brought a variety of all of Sweet's favorite candy, jumped on the 52 bus to Misericordia Hospital on Cedar Ave.

When I walked through the revolving door I couldn't help but notice the receptionist at the front desk was drop dead gorgeous. Her skin was smooth and rich like dark chocolate with not one bump or blemish and she had the sexiest mole right above her lip. She was a few years older than me but I wasn't at all intimidated. "How may I help you?" She had no idea how much I was admiring her. Using my proper voice and Yale manners, I replied,

"Yes you can. Could you tell me what room Samantha Wilson is in?"

She started clicking around on her computer until she found her name.

" Samantha Wilson, oh yea, she's in room 942."

"May I have a visitors pass please?"

She got the pass and put Sweet's name and room number on it.

As she handed me the visitor's pass I pulled one of the long stem roses from the dozen and handed it to her. She accepted it. Smelling the rose she smiled.

"Why didn't you give me the whole dozen?"

I leaned over her desk to look into her eyes.

"Because one is special like you."

She smiled and sniffed the rose again as I walked away towards the elevator door. I thought to myself, "Sorry Sweets but that one was too fine to overlook."

On the elevator my heart started racing not knowing what to expect in Sweet's room. I imagined Sweet's family waiting in the room ready to beat me down or I thought the police might have intimidated her into telling them who the driver of the stolen car really was. Either way I had to see her.

When I got to room 942 I paused, took a deep breath, and walked into her room. She was alone and asleep with an IV coming from her arm. She had two black eyes and her nose appeared to be broken by the way it was wrapped. Her silky hair had a white bandage around it and her left cheek had a big gauze pad on it. She also had on a neck brace and a cast on her right arm. She looked pretty bad off.

I walked over to her and I gently touched her hand that didn't have the cast on it and her eyes opened slowly. I heard my heart racing inside of my chest. I felt horrible about what I did to Sweets. I got on my knees next to the head of her bed.

"I'm sorry Sweets baby. I couldn't stop. I lost control. I... I..."

"Awe stop bitchin with your non-driving ass.

I reached down and pulled her up to hold her. We both broke out into tears. Sweets was what I call a soap and water beauty. Pretty skin, pretty hair, perfect teeth and a cover girl physique. She always said she wanted to be a model.

I gave her the flowers and candy and wiped both of our eyes with the same napkin.

"Can you put the flowers in that vase and open a now and later and put it in my mouth."

"Sure Sweets, anything you want."

I did exactly as she requested.

"G you messed me up real bad."

Wiping the tears from her eyes with the back of my hand.

"I know Sweets baby."

She pushed my hand away from her face.

"What I want to know is why you ain't hurt?"

I sat up and pounded myself on the chest.

"Because I'm a karate man and karate men hurt on the inside."

She laughed holding her cheek.

"Stop making me laugh. That shit hurts."

Then her face got serious again.

"Hey G, my moms and uncle are on their way up here to see me and they probably wouldn't be happy to see you although I told them it wasn't you in the car during the crash but my cousin Bee Bee saw us together and told her the truth."

Now Case always said that things that you do in life always come out one way or another. If it doesn't come out in the wash, it comes out in the rinse.

"So how long are you going to be in here?"

"Probably for a week or so."

I reached in my pocket and counted my money. It was $215. I lifted her up enough to put the money under her pillow.

"I'm going to leave now since your people are coming up. Here's money for your phone and T.V., page me if you need anything."

She tried to smile but it looked painful.

"Thanks G."

I gave her a soft kiss on her forehead and headed towards the door.

"Hey G wait!"

I stopped dead in my tracks.

"Before you leave, pass me my pocketbook."

I walked back to her night table and handed it to her. She reached inside slowly, obviously in pain.

"Here, take this," handing me a weekly bus transpass.

"What's this for?"

"Stay on the bus until your no-skill having ass learns how to drive."

She laughed holding her face again. I took the transpass, gave her another hug, and left.

When I returned my visitors pass to the receptionist she handed me a small piece of paper. I opened it and seen that it was her phone number.

"I still want a dozen," she said smiling.

"Don't play with me girl. I'll be planting an orchard tomorrow," I said as I slid her number in my pocket and headed for the double doors.

Damn. Sweets is a real trooper, I thought.

She can roll with me anytime. I'll have to buy her something real special when she comes home.

If These Streets Could Talk

CH 7 The Big Payback

As soon as I walked through my door my pager went off. It was Shank. I knew it was him because he uses code 007 like he's a secret agent or something. I called him right back.

"Did you hit me Shank?"

He sounded pretty upset.

"No man the question is what in the hell did you hit? You destroyed my best-stolen piece. I rode by and saw that Z28 wrapped around that beam so tight that they might as well leave it there as a memorial. Plus I heard that you damn near killed Sweets."

" Alright man, you don't have to rub it in. I already feel bad enough."

"Well luckily she's alright because I still want to get some of that little fine young thing."

" Shank I told you before that Sweets is off limits."

"Man you kill me with that off limits shit. I know Sweets just as well as you do. I'll just buy her a nice outfit, get her hair and nails done, and then have those legs behind her head like rabbit ears."

Now I started to get mad.

"Yea well Sweets ain't going out like that. Plus I taught her better than that. She knows that if she needs **anything** she can get it from me."

"You know what kills me about you G? You buy Sweets clothes, take her out to dinner, she even spends the night over your house from time to time and you never even tried to get none of that ass as good as she looks. Can I ask you something personal G, are you gay?"

"Why don't you ask your sister if I'm gay."

He didn't like me saying that since he knew I had slept with his sister on plenty occasions.

"Look Shank, Sweets is like a little sister to me and I'm prepared to protect her like one at any cost so don't try to play her."

I sensed that Shank didn't like my aggressive approach so he switched the conversation back to the car.

"Well anyway, what are you going to do about reimbursing me for my ride Mr. Cock Blocker?"

"I'll pay you back Shank, just give me a minute."

"Yea well that's all you got is a minute. Remember the clock is tickin."

He hung up.

For the next few weeks I had to hustle my but off. Shank wanted me to pay him $3,000 for a car that wasn't even his but I had to pay him. Then on top of selling weed I was cutting grass, bagging groceries, cleaning basements, basically doing anything for cash. I knew Shank wouldn't go to the police but his reputation was on the line. You see in the hood we have a code of silence. If it's not any of your business, you stay out of it. Even though the whole neighborhood knew that I was the driver of that stolen car nobody told the police in fear of retaliation. Snitches get stitches where I'm from.

A few weeks later Sweets was released from the hospital. I greeted her at the hospital exit with balloons, a bag of all of her favorite candy, and a brand new Gloria Vanderbilt denim outfit.

"G you didn't have to do all of this," she said snatching the bags out of my hand. "But then again yes you did."

We hugged and kissed.

"Man can we go to Mickey D's or something, I'm hungry as a runaway slave. That hospital crap made me feel sicker than I was."

"Yea Sweets, anything you want."

If These Streets Could Talk

Little did she know my pockets were low after paying off Shank. It was hard getting the money up but I did it. Me and Sweets had a lot of catching up to do so we walked to 52nd St. and caught the 52 bus to Mc Donald's.

If These Streets Could Talk

Chapter 8 Thou Shall Not Steal

The summer of '82'. The hot designer clothing was Izod, Gloria Vanderbilt, Chardon, and Gazells and I didn't possess any of that stuff. It seemed like I never recovered financially after paying Shank off. He on the other hand got a kick out of me working so hard to pay him back.

In high school peer pressure is at an all time high to be with the so called "in crowd" that if you didn't have the latest styles and fashions, you were a nobody.

Although KK couldn't really afford it she sent me back to Delaware Valley High to finish my high school diploma. KK had four kids in private school and she made it very clear that she wasn't buying any designer clothing. "Besides," she would say, "white people don't wear that stuff." Well I wasn't rich or white and I had to have it.

I had two other buddies in my click named Stoney and Rich. They were brothers and they were "boosters" (professional shoplifters). If it wasn't bolted down, they would steal it. I mean they had all the latest designer fashions and I wanted in so they decided to take me to Gimbals department store with them on one of their missions.

Stoney would keep the salesman busy pretending to be interested in purchasing something while Rich would take as many items as he could into the fitting room and start getting dressed. He had a skinny-framed body like me so he would start putting on extra small sizes and work his way up to extra large ones. He would put all of the clothing on his slender body and when he came out of the dressing room, he would look like a fat boy. Then on the way out of the store he would stuff a few large bottles of expensive perfume and cologne into his pockets. It was too easy. I had to be in.

If These Streets Could Talk

After a while I learned how to become a fat boy too. I even got so good at it that I started asking people around the neighborhood what did they want me to bring back from the store. You know, like placing orders. I got so good at it that I would bring back whatever people requested and sell the merchandise for half of the ticket price.

In time I became a walking clothing store. Also in time Stoney and Rich got a little jealous because I was stealing and selling more then the two of them put together. Soon they tried to extort me for my money. I was sort of intimidated since they were a little older then me.

At first I would give them a couple of dollars here and there for showing me the ropes on how to steal. Then they started demanding half of my take making threats about what they were going to do to me if I didn't cooperate. I told Case about them trying to muscle my hustle and he had a little talk with them with his two .45 calibers pointed at their heads. They never asked me for another dime.

I was the sharpest kid in the 10th grade wearing all different colored Izod shirts and designer jeans. My boys worked with me. We stole so much from the Center City department stores that the security got too tight so we moved our business to the suburbs.

In the suburbs shoplifting was even easier. The last thing the sales person thinks is that you're stealing. Since most people in the burbs already had money they didn't have to steal. It was just too classy of an area. They were **too** gullible. We would make two, sometimes three trips back to different stores just changing our clothes and hats to disguise ourselves.

The clothing business was going really well except for one problem. I was my best customer. I just loved the attention I was getting from all of the girls for noticing my vast wardrobe since I hardly ever wore the same thing twice. I was wearing more than I was selling.

Then Rich got caught one day and spent three months in the juvenile detention center. After that me and Stoney got a little nervous and stopped boosting.

I had another buddy name Race. He introduced us to stickups and burglaries. At first I was afraid of holding a gun but as time went on and the power I felt when people totally submitted whatever they had to me when I put my pistol to their head and told them my little stick up line, "It's only a robbery, don't make it a murder," really started to turn me on.

We started off doing petty crimes like victimizing drunks coming out of bars late at night or robbing people coming out of the bank or check cashing place. Stony and Rich would also rob old ladies but that wasn't my cup of tea. They called me a punk but I always had a special respect for women, especially older ones. I always thought about how I would feel if someone robbed my mother or sisters.

Next we started robbing drug dealers. We figured what were they going to do, call the cops and tell them somebody stole their cocaine or weed money. They would have to just grin and bear it.

We knew about these kids down 32nd Street, a small drug infested area in West Philly better known as "The Bottom." They were getting a lot of money on this small block. Rich had just come home from juvenile and our cash flow was low.

"I'm tellin ya'll man," Stoney said.

"Toot and them is rippin it down 32nd St. I hear their dope house is pullin in between $20,000 to $30,000 a day. All we got to do is show them boys this 44 Magnum and they will be shittin in their draws givin up the money."

"I don't know man. Them boys down there are crazy. They don't care about life itself. I seen Toot crack some dudes teeth out with a 2 x 4 for $15 he owed him. Plus he's cock diesel from lifting all of those weights in the pen."

"Man I don't give a fuck about all that muscle bound shit!."
Holding his .44 magnum in the air.

Like Kool G rap said, "Sylvester Stalone ain't shit against Al Capone!" One of these little bullets can take down a 400-pound nigga. And don't you sound like a little bitch. "He has big muscles," Who gives a shit! What you need to do is man up! Now you want some real money or what?"

Rich looked over at me.

" He's right G. I just got home from the joint and I'm broke as a joke, so what's up? Whatcha gonna do?"

I sat there and thought for a second.

"Well if ya'll are down, I'm down." We all gave each other a brotherhood handshake and hug. I knew after that there was no turning back.

Deep down inside I didn't really want to be down but once again I let peer pressure get the best of me.

For the next three days the three of us would ride down 32nd St. in a stolen car plotting on how we were going to rob Toots gang. We parked our car on the corner and watched as their customers would walk up to one guy and give him the money. Using hand signals he would signal another guy across the street from him how much drugs to give the customer. This person in turn would go across the street and signal another person looking down from an abandon house in the middle of the block. The look out person would drop the package from out of the window. The runner would then give the drugs to the buyer. This was an on going process. Our only concern was the moneyman. He was our key focus.

The following night we sat parked across the street from the activities in one of Shanks stolen cars. Customers were coming nonstop.

"Ya'll see that? Only one guy collects the money" Stoney said while smoking a joint. "We put the pistol to his head, get the money, and be out. It's as simple as that."

Rich leaned over and took the joint from Stoney.

"Let's do this."

The next evening we parked the car in the middle of the block. Stoney and Rich were smoking a joint. Rich tried to pass it to me.

"Naw man I'm cool, I don't want none."

Little did they know that my stomach was in knots because I had a bad feeling about this one.

As usual Stoney had the gun.

"Alright G, I'll throw the pistol to his head while you take the cash. Rich, you keep the motor running and we'll be right back. Here."

Throwing me a ski mask.

"What's this for?"

"Just put it on. That big ass head of yours is too recognizable."

The two of them laughed and under normal circumstances I would have too, but tonight I didn't think nothing was funny.

It was about 2:00 am and it had just stopped raining. The streets were damp and dark and the wind had a cutting chill to it.

As we walked down the street we had saw moneyman in view. I walked nervously behind Stoney as he was focused strictly on moneyman with that familiar cold look in his eye he always had when we were about to do some dirt. Like he had ice water in his veins.

As we were nearing our target I saw some guy step out of a house across the street. Me and him caught each other's eye and then he eased back into the building. I tried to tell Stoney about the guy but he started walking faster.

"Come on G, keep up!"

We approached moneyman. He was tall, thin and dark skinned wearing a goose down coat wide open to show off his thick gold rope chain.

"What do ya'll niggas need?" He said licking his thumbs counting his money not even looking up at us. Stoney reached into his inside coat pocket and pulled out his long .44 Magnum.

"What the fuck do you think we need?" Putting the gun to Moneyman's head while snatching his gold rope chain off of his neck.

Moneyman's eyes looked like he had seen a ghost as he dropped his stack of money on the damp pavement.

"Alright man, take it but please don't shoot me."

Stoney gave me a push in the back.

"Do it!" He demanded me.

I went over to Moneyman and started searching his pockets with my hands shaking wildly. He was loaded with money in every pocket. I patted him down and found money rolled up in rubber bands in his sox, a knot in his pants, and wads in every pocket of his jacket.

"Hurry up and get what's on the ground!" Stoney demanded as he held his gun to Moneyman's forehead while confiscating his gold rings and watch.

When I bent down to pick up the money I noticed Money man's jeans were saturated with urine. He just didn't know I was as nervous as he was.

I got on my knees picking up the wet dollar bills from off of the damp street. As I rose up I saw a shadow behind Stoney. At first I thought it was Rich but when I stood up completely I realized that it was the kid I had seen ducking back in the house from in the middle of the block. He had a pistol pointed at the back of Stoney's head. Before I could open my mouth, "BLAM ! BLAM!"

Stoney dropped face down. All I could see was the back of his head completely blown off, as his body went down like a rag-doll. His nerves made him involuntarily flip on his back and his eyes were rolled up in his head and his entire body was shaking hysterically.

Moneyman took off running and screaming like a girl. My mind was telling me to run but my feet felt like they had cement in them. I was in shock and total disbelief. I looked down as Stoney's body stopped shaking and he took what appeared to be his last breath.

The unknown assassin then pointed the gun at me. I knew in my heart that I was dead so I just closed my eyes and awaited the fatal shot.

He pointed the gun at my head and squeezed the trigger and nothing happened. I opened my eyes and looked at him. He quickly pulled back the chamber, aimed the gun at my head again and squeezed. Again nothing happened. (There goes my angel again). All of a sudden I shook the cement off of my feet and took off running like I was shot out of a cannon. I almost fell over my own feet. I ran so fast that it felt like I was hydroplaning.

Running towards me was Rich.

"Rich go back, we got to get out of here!" I yelled frightfully running towards him while snatching the sky mask off of my face.

"Where's Stoney?"

"He's gone man, we got to go!"

"What the fuck do you mean he's gone?" Rich said with a worried look on his face.

We ran past each other in opposite directions as I headed for the car and he ran towards his brother. I jumped into the drivers' seat and heard three more shots. I yanked the car into drive and peeled off sideswiping parked cars as I skidded down the street. I ducked as I heard three more shots hit the rear of our stolen car.

I took the car to Fairmont Park where we had another stolen car waiting in the woods. Then as previously planned, I deuced the shot up car with gasoline, and torched it, jumped in the other car, then drove straight to Case's apartment on the first floor and told him everything that had just taken place.

"What the hell is wrong with you?" he yelled as he smacked me in my head.

"I grew up down the bottom and if word gets out that my little brother did some stupid shit like this, I'm going to have to go to war with those boys. You know those cats down there don't play that dumb shit."

"Stony and Rich are gone."

I was crying and my body was shaking uncontrollably. I started hyperventilating.

Smacking me again, "You're damned right they're gone. You're lucky that your dumb ass ain't gone too."

Case took a long hard drag from his cigarette and blew out a huge cloud of smoke. "All right this is what you do. I want you to lay low for a few days until this thing surfaces and I'll find out what the word is on the streets. Hopefully that mask protected you from being recognized.

He took another long drag from his cigarette.

"Meanwhile, break me down with some of that blood money."

With everything that had just taken place I had forgotten that I had the money so I pulled it out and we counted it. It was $6,300. I gave Case half and crept upstairs to my apartment and got into bed.

I had nightmares that evening thinking about Stoney's brains being blown out right in front of me. I don't think Stoney realized it at the time but I was glad he gave me that ski mask since no one ever found out who the little masked fella was. He indirectly saved my life.

At Stoney and Rich's funeral, **all** of our friends were present and heart broken. It was the first time someone in our click had gotten killed, but it wouldn't be the last. They had to carry my boys mom out on a stretcher because she fainted from viewing their bodies. Loosing her only two sons at the same time was too much for her to handle. Case always said, "You live fast, you die young, you make a beautiful corpse."

I never told anyone that I was present when it all happened. That was me and Case's little secret.

A couple of guys at the funeral were talking about getting revenge on the guys down the Bottom but deep down inside everyone knew that the two dead brothers were destined to go out the way they did. You live by the sword, you die by the sword. You live by the gun, you die by the gun.

After Stony and Rich's death I decided to go back to school. KK sent me back to Delaware Valley High trying to keep me out of the neighborhood as much as possible because I had some catching up to do. But of course I needed a winter wardrobe so I went to Case to get some weed on credit to start selling.

I started selling $5.00 bags around the neighborhood on my bicycle. I became the weed delivery boy. People would call my pager and I would meet them with the weed.

For the next two years I went to school non-stop. From September to June, then from June to September. In the summertime, Jones and my other friends would be outside late at night drinking beer and smoking weed while I was in the house studying. Case told me to get an education because once you get the knowledge in your head, can't nobody take it away from you. And I did it. Class of "84". All of my friends would laugh at me going to summer school until I was walking down that graduation aisle and they weren't. It really felt good.

After graduation KK bribed me into joining the Marine Corp. She said she would rent me a car for the entire summer and send me on a nice trip if I agreed to sign up by September. Since I wasn't going to college she wanted me to do something with my life.

I thought about how much I hated studying in High School and I wasn't looking forward to going to college any time soon, so I agreed to join the Marine Corp in September. What was I thinking?

If These Streets Could Talk

Ch 9 Uncle Sam

"You've got ten seconds to get the hell off of my bus and you've already wasted three!" The Drill Instructor yelled as he jumped on the school bus packed with new recruits.

Paris Island, South Carolina, United States Marine Corp. What in the hell did I get myself into? Me, Jones, and my life long buddy John signed up to join the Marine Corp together on the buddy system. That's when you and a friend or two join the military together and your suppose to stay together throughout the duration of your tour. What a joke.

Jones' parents canceled his contract a few days before we were shipped off to boot camp. His father knew a committeeman or something down City Hall so it was just John and me and we were scared to death. It was dark, hot, damp, and the big drill instructors with the Smokey the Bear hats didn't make the atmosphere any more pleasant.

If you have seen the movie Full Metal Jacket, than you've been to Marine Corps basic training. They shave your head suit you up, then the brain washing begins. They want you to sleep, eat, and breath Marine corp. I was ignorant to the fact that I could have gone to college through grants, scholarships, and other financial aid. KK had me under the impression that I couldn't go to college since she didn't have the money to send me. I guess she was ignorant to, so off to the Corps I went.

There were a lot of things the Corps taught me. Some of them were self-discipline, self-pride, self-respect, and the importance of physical conditioning. Another was to never volunteer for anything.

If These Streets Could Talk

In basic training they turned my body into a machine. In just sixteen weeks I went from 140 lb. of skin and bones to a 170 lb. lean, mean, killing machine of pure muscle. I mean I had non-stop energy. But believe me it was no easy ride getting there. Basic training was pure torture. The saying "We do more before 6:00 am than most people do all day," was no exaggeration.

Our day would start between the hours of 3:00 am and 4:00 am. They would literally throw us out of our bunks while we were asleep yelling and throwing trashcans down the middle of the squad bay until everyone was out of their bunk. Then we had to perform what our drill instructors called the triple "S"s. Shit, shower, and shave. Then they would run us through the showers like cattle. You would have to wash your entire body in 60 seconds. They would tell us to hit the hot spots. Then we would have to jump into our clothes, clean the entire squad bay and make our bunks to perfection. Our sheets had to have forty-five degree angles and a twelve-inch fold. Our blankets would have to be so tightly wrapped around our mattresses that you could bounce a coin off of them. We would run to the cafeteria in formation where we were forced to wolf down our breakfast in record time. The last person to eat was the squad leader. When he was done eating everyone had to leave, finished or not.

We would take a class learning from our military handbook and afterwards we were made to run a few miles. Sounds impossible in three hours? Well it wasn't because we did it, daily. Then for the rest of the day we would attend school and practice survival tactics and hand to hand combat preparing us for war situations.

There were two things that drill instructors hated. The first was killing sand fleas. It was totally unacceptable.

If These Streets Could Talk

Sand fleas were very small flying insects with an extremely painful bite. I never knew of their existence until I went to South Carolina. Their bite was similar to being stuck with a needle.

I once saw a private get caught smacking one off of his neck. Our drill instructor actually made him dig a six-foot grave and conduct a funeral service for the sand fleas. Is that ridiculous or what? But believe me it was effective. After witnessing that the rest of us just took those bites from those little bugs and kept on moving.

The second thing drill instructors hated were people from Philly and NY. They accused us of being slick and undisciplined and they were right. Believe me I killed my share of sand fleas every time they turned their back. Plus being from Philly or NY made them ride us a little harder than the other guys. For instance in the smoke and gas chamber. They would keep us in there a little longer to so call teach our slick butts a lesson.

The gas chamber was an experience all in itself. We would enter this dark gloomy looking room. In it, our captain would be inside wearing what looked like a biohazard chemical all white suite and mask giving us the "I got a little surprise for you," look.

You could actually see the fumes from the chemical mixture inside of beaker going to work.

The smoke coming from the beaker would slowly surround the small airtight room. Looking around the room at everyone's eyes, I realized that I wasn't the only one scared to death. They would make us run in place for about one minute to get our heart rates up assuring we get a good intake of the mild toxic gas. Then came the removal of the mask where people totally freaked out. I mean the biggest, strongest guys fell to their knees and started crying, gagging, and rolling around on the ground like a dog after being hit by a car.

If These Streets Could Talk

Although my eyes were burning too, seeing those other guys acting like they were dying was hilarious. I was laughing and crying at the same time. Then after staying in the chamber for about 60 seconds, although it felt like an eternity, we had to exit the chamber holding our masks in the air and saying our social security numbers and believe me that was no easy task. Recruits were coughing and gagging and rubbing their eyes, which was the worst thing to do because for some reason when you rub your eyes, it felt like someone rubbing sand into them. Some guys had snot coming from their noses down to their boots and the ones who didn't say their social security numbers got tossed right back into the steel door.

I was barely able to blurt out my social security number from all of the gagging and coughing I was doing. "What did you say boy. I can't understand you," the Drill Instructor said pointing at the gas chamber door threatening to throw me back in. I took a deep breath and repeated it slowly so he could understand me, 146-22-7381. He just pushed me looking disappointed that I got it right. "Keep up boy."

John was right behind me but he wasn't so lucky. He was coughing and gagging so much until he vomited on the Drill Instructor's boots. Big mistake.

"Boy you must have lost your god-dam mind!" He grabbed Jon kicking and screaming and dragged him back towards the chamber door.

" No Sir, please don't make me go back in there," John pleaded as he was being dragged by both of his legs kicking and screaming. The Drill Instructor just ignored him and threw him back in. All we could hear was Jon banging on the steel doors.

"Noooo, noooo, noooooo......." Until the screams faded away.

When they finally dragged him out, he had snot and vomit all over him. A few of us dragged him back to the barracks and threw him in the shower. I kind of laughed to myself about the whole thing since around the "W" John was a tough guy. Now he's just crying like a little lost puppy. If only the fellas could see him like this, they wouldn't believe it.

Marine Corp boot camp had to have been the most difficult task I have ever been forced to accomplish. It was physically and mentally draining. They would mentally torment you to see if you would crack under the pressure. The only thing that kept me going was my homeboy John. Although he was physically fit and academically intelligent, he was the most uncoordinated person that I have ever seen. He would constantly get thrown out of formation when we were marching because he would be on his left foot when everyone else was on their right. I never knew he was so uncoordinated since he was so athletic.

Part of our physical was going to the optometrist to see who needed glasses. When those who needed glasses prescriptions were ready they made the rest of us line up on two sides facing each other while the glasses wearing marines marched between us.

The other guys looked a little funny marching by but I didn't really know them but when I saw John with that bald egg shaped head and those Drew Cary glasses, I lost it. I tried to hold my laugh so hard that snot shot out of my nose and I burst into an unrestrained laughter. My Drill Instructor couldn't believe it.

"Pizarro, what in the hell is your major malfunction boy!"

Trying to straighten up and wipe the smile off of my face and the snot from my nose because I knew I was in major trouble.

"Nothing Sir!"

"Who gave you permission to laugh in my formation!"

"No one Sir!"

"Who gave you permission to shoot snot out of your nasty nose in my formation boy!"

"No one Sir!"

"Get your retarded ass up here right now front and center!"

I ran up to my Drill Instructor at top speed and stood nervously at attention.

"Now you tell me what in the hell is so funny boy or I'm going to beat you like a circus animal!"

"Sir, the private never seen an egg with glasses before, sir!" I said pointing at John. The entire squad bay started laughing which was a big mistake.

"Shut up that dog gone laughing," my Drill Instructor turned around and barked at the rest of the privates. All laughing ceased immediately.

Then he was suspiciously calm all of a sudden.

"So, since private Pizarro here wants to be a comedian and you girls are his audience, hell we might as well all play together. Grab your swim trunks, shower shoes, and towels. Girls, we're going to the beach." And he walked away whistling.

Now I knew darn well we weren't going to the beach but I also knew that wherever it was, wouldn't be nice.

He marched us behind our barracks to a big sand pit. One of our Drill Instructors was already there with a garden hose hosing down the sand.

It was close to 100 degrees outside and they exercised us in that wet sand pit for what seemed like forever. Leg lifts, six inches, then ninety inches, push ups, squat- thrusts, digging, running in place, you name it, and they called it out. The whole time talking trash to us.

"Don't you ladies look cute in your bathing suits," making sure he pushed my face down into the sand a little more than the other privates. It was a dirty painful experience.

When they were finished humiliating us, they made us run back to the squad bay with our faces full of sand and our bodies sore. I had total muscle failure. That's when you're so physically exhausted you can't even raise your hands above your head.

That evening I felt a lot of animosity towards me in the barracks. I didn't sleep all night long in fear of a blanket party, (That's where they roll you up in your blanket while your asleep and everyone beats the crap out of you) but luckily my angel protected me through the night.

We only had four weeks left of physical and mental torture before we graduated from boot camp and, we were pumped up. All of the working out and exercise really paid off. I felt and looked stronger than ever. When they exercised us, it didn't hurt anymore and the five-mile runs weren't as strenuous. Although we thought exercise was punishment, they were just building our bodies up and they did a good job doing it.

We were in class one day when a sergeant from the office interrupted our class to make an announcement.

"All right listen up! Nikiski, Forson, Reveria, and Pizarro, front and center." The four of us ran up to the front of the class and stood at attention.

"You four maggots follow me," he said as walked out of the door. I thought what the heck did I do now.

He marched us to the barracks.
"Alright you four terds. Shower up, spit shine your boots and put on a clean uniform. You all are going to see the Sergeant Major."

If These Streets Could Talk

The four of us were baffled not knowing why we were singled out from everyone else.

I was sitting on my bunk after showering putting on my uniform when my senior drill instructor came up to me. Sergeant Norwood was about 5'7", very dark in complexion and very stocky with 0% body fat. I was shining my boots when he walked up on me. I immediately jumped to attention.

"At ease," he said giving me a disgusted look.

"Pizarro, what did you do, eat that stuff for lunch?"

I jumped to attention looking at him confused, " Excuse me sir".

" I said what did you do, eat marijuana for lunch? Your piss test showed so much THC in your system that the chemist got a buzz."

He took off his Smoky the Bear hat and sat on my bunk.

"Now Pizarro, there's something about you that I like and that's rare. I've been watching how hard you work. You have a lot of potential to become a good Marine and I hate seeing that go down the drain. Now you listen to me. When you go see the Sergeant Major you better convince him that you want to be a Marine because they have you and those other three numb nuts down as drug frauds and you know that that's an immediate discharge."

I was in shock. After all of this they want to discharge me for smoking a joint. This was the first time in my life that KK and the rest of my family were proud of me and I wasn't about to let them down. That would mean I would have to go home a disgrace, a failure, and I wasn't about to let that happen. I didn't care if I had to literally kiss somebody's butt with my lips; I wasn't going home without that dress blue uniform on. I also couldn't figure out why they didn't catch John. To my recollection he smoked way more weed than I did.

On the way to the Sergeant Major's office I thought back at the going away party that my family and friends threw for me and John down my basement. On top of all of the alcohol that I consumed I did recall smoking about two joints. I couldn't believe after all of the hell they put us through they wanted to throw us out of boot camp. They should have had our drug test results before we were enlisted.

"Sergeant Major. Here are the drug frauds as you requested," Sergeant Norwood introduced us.

"Carry on."

Sergeant Norwood gave me the eye as he did an about face and left the room.

Our sergeant major was a older very stern looking man. His gray hair was cut into a box shape to match his square jaw line. He had to be near sixty years old but his chest stood out further than his stomach and his tattoos on his forearm said USMC.

Around his office you could see all of his military achievement awards and accomplishments. He had pictures of Vietnam and other war paraphernalia.

The four of us were standing at attention lined up like we were at the police line-up. He first walked up to Nikiski reading from something that appeared to be a file.

"So junkie, what kind of dope did you pump into your body before trying to get into my Marine Corp?"

Nikiski was a white guy from upstate Pennsylvania and just from his physical appearance I could tell he was a pure burnout. His eyes were always red and he talked with very slurred speech. I assumed that he was high every time I seen him.

Barely standing at attention, "Well Sir, I did some valium, some ruthies, some crack, a little coke, some opium, some zanex, some....."

Sergeant Major cut him off.

"That's enough you walking germ! Get the hell out of my office before you make me puke! It feels like I'm getting high just looking at your ass you walking pharmacy!"

Nikiski ran out of the office slamming the door behind him.

Next was Forson a kind of quiet guy from Ohio. Sergeant major looked him up and down.

"So pea brain, what's your addiction?"

Forson nervously cleared his throat. He had a hard country accent.

" Sir, I did some heroin the day before boot camp. My daddy made me join the Corp. because he was a Marine and his daddy and his daddy before him was a Marine. He said it was in our blood line."

Suddenly he burst into tears.

"I wanted to be a nurse but he wouldn't let me. He says that I am destined to be a Marine. Please sir, could I just go home. I don't want to be here anymore."

Sergeant Major grabbed him by the collar threw him to the ground.

"Get out of here you faggot before I stomp you to death you sorry piece of shit!" He picked himself up and ran out the door.

Next was me. Sergeant Major walked up to me. I stuck my chest out and looked straight ahead.

"So what are you a crack head? Or maybe you shoot heroin too."

"No Sir," I interrupted. "Neither," I expressed with a stern voice. "Sir, the private just smoked a joint one week before boot camp which was a stupid thing to do but has every intention of becoming a dedicated Marine, Sir!"

"Not smoking pot you won't."

"Sir all of my life I wanted to stand for something and nothing makes me more proud than to wear this uniform, Sir!"

He walked up closer to me and put his face so close to mine that our noses were touching. His cigar breath made me want to vomit.

"Boy you just gave me a hard on. If you mean that I'm going to give you the privilege to stay in my Corp. But if you do as much as look at another drug I'm going to rip off your head and shit down your neck do you here me boy?"

"Sir yes Sir!"

I breathed a sigh of relief as he walked over to Reveria.

Next was Reveria, a pretty boy from Brooklyn. I don't check out guys but he was a pretty boy. He had real sharp facial features, thick black eyebrows and hazel eyes. Every night at mail call he would get 5 to 10 letters from different pretty girls with pictures in every envelope.

He told the Sergeant Major that he too had only smoked a joint and was given permission to stay in the Corp.

From that day until we graduated me and Reveria were referred to as drug frauds. Whenever there was a mess detail, they would call me and Reveria the drug frauds. Whenever they needed a volunteer, they would call the drug frauds, which was all right with us because we were happy just to stay in the Corps. We both left the office relieved.

After that me and Reveria became very close friends. In fact after basic training we both got orders to get shipped to Camp Lejune North Carolina. Our M.O.S. (military operational skill) was 0347 Automotive Mechanics.

After graduating from basic training John and me went home on leave for ten days and what a relief. When we landed at the Philadelphia International Airport we got a heroes welcome from our family and some friends at the gates. I looked and felt so proud in that dress blue uniform. You can't beat the respect and attention you get in a military uniform.

When we got on the "W" things seemed a little different. The first thing I noticed was Cases weed business had sky rocketed. He was selling so much weed out of the first floor of KK's building you would think he had a license to do so. Then I found out KK wasn't complaining because of the hush money she received from him every week.

When I walked into his apartment I was astonished. There was the biggest T.V that I had ever seen sitting in the middle of the floor. He had money green Italian leather furniture and a digital state of the art stereo system. He was always a flashy dresser but it seemed like his wardrobe stepped up two notches. I looked around the living room in amazement.

"Damn Case, your weed business is really blowing up."

Smoking a joint and looking at me nonchalantly,

"Yeah, I must admit that I'm eating pretty good these days but look at you Mr. Marine. You're looking extra sharp in that uniform and I'm proud of you. You even picked up a few muscles on the way."

He blew out a huge cloud of smoke.

" Now use Uncle Sam to your advantage and make something of yourself. Go to school while you're in there and come out with a degree. Don't let this little bit of flash that you see around here fool you. It's not as sweet as it looks."

Just then the doorbell rang and before Case could open it Jones busted in.

"Yo Case, I need some more weed," he stopped when he seen me, "Yo G my brother what's up?"

He ran over to me and hugged me lifting me off of my feet checking out my uniform.

" Look at you dude."

"No man, look at you," I said impressively.

Jones was looking like new money from head to toe. FILA hat, FILA sweat suit, FILA sneakers, and the biggest, thickest gold rope chain that I had ever seen around his neck.

" Dam Jones, how are you living man?"

Brushing off his sleeves with the back of his hands then grabbing the diamond letter J he had around his neck,

"Large G, plain old large. Come outside, let me show you something."

Outside in front of the apartment building, Jones had a customized Cadillac Seville, loaded. He even had a speakerphone built into the sun visor.

"Check this out," he said as we both got into the car.

He turned on the stereo, "BOOM!, BOOM!

"Jones, who put this system in?"

Trying to yell over the music, "Wait, I'm not finished."

He pushed a small button on the equalizer and the stereo went up about ten more decibels making the car windows sound like they were going to shatter. Then he turned the music down so we could talk.

"G man Case got this weed thing on lock. We be sellin so much that we can't keep up. It's like he put some comeback in it or something.

He lit up a joint.

"I'm glad you did the right thing by going into the service," he said while smoking the joint smiling.

"Yeah," I said with a feeling of uncertainty, "me to." Thinking back at how his parents got him out of enlisting.

If These Streets Could Talk

My ten-day home visit went so fast but it was fun seeing the gang again. Plus my newly formed body got me a lot of attention from the girls but the only one I had my eye on was Yalanna Knight. I always had a crush on her but she was four years younger than me. I also admired the fact that she went to school faithfully and was an honor roll student. Case instilled in me to stay away from pretty airhead girls and Yalanna was no airhead.

Yalanna was caramel brown complexion with shoulder length hair, brown eyes, and when she smiled she had the deepest dimples in her cheeks. Yalanna also had the body of a grown woman and carried it well. She lived a few blocks away from me but always walked through the "W" to catch the train. She also had a walk that made other girls hate her. Once I got her phone number I knew she would be mine.

Yalanna and I spent a lot of time together before I went down to North Carolina. So much time Yalanna lost her virginity to me before I left. A few of my boys were jealous because they tried several times just to get her phone number and failed.

The evening before I was to fly to North Carolina I assured her that she was my girl and when I came home for good I'd marry her and buy her a big house.

"G, I know you're going to be around a lot of woman while you're on your tour of duty but can you promise me one thing?"

"Anything baby?"

"Promise me that you don't make any babies out there because I want to have yours."

I put my finger under her chin and pulled her face close to mine while looking her straight in her eyes.

"First of all, I could never forget you. Secondly, I can't make any babies because I had my tubes tied."

She laughed playfully punching me in the stomach "Well you'd better untie them when I'm ready to have one."

"Consider it done," I said as I kissed her soft full lips.

When we made love that night I truly fell in love. For me to only be nineteen years old I'd been with quite a few girls but none like Yalanna. I could actually feel the love in our lovemaking. I could also tell by her involuntary body jerks and astonished facial expression that the feeling was mutual.

If These Streets Could Talk

Ch 10 Let The Games Begin

It was time for me to leave. When my flight arrived in North Carolina I felt like I was in another world. The people at the airport were friendly and smiling and would actually speak to you, unlike Philly. In Philly most people won't even look at you if they don't know or recognize you. "The City of Brotherly Love." (What a joke).

When I arrived on base I noticed the atmosphere was a lot more relaxed than boot camp. Everybody was kind of doing his or her own thing and they would tease those of us who were fresh out of boot camp with our high and tight haircuts.

When I got to my barracks I heard a familiar voice.

"Que Pasa Pizarro."

I turned around and saw my homeboy Reveria.

"What's up devil dog," I said as we embraced. We hugged each other Marine Corp style.

"Come down here S- A. I reserved a top bunk for you just the way you like homes."

"Lead the way amigo," I tried to playfully trip him as I walked behind him.

Our barracks had about thirty bunks so that meant that I had sixty roommates. Reveria had been there for three or four days before me so he wanted to show me the ropes and I couldn't wait to find out.

First we ate at the chow hall then he took me to the enlisted club or E Club as it was called. It was a bar for enlisted men like ourselves where you could drink, shoot pool, and listen to live musical bands. Then he took me out into town to the mall and all of the hot spots like where the prostitutes and drug heads hung out. He also showed me the hottest disco in Jacksonville N.C, The Galaxy. I felt like it was the new beginning for me in this new town.

If These Streets Could Talk

Once you get out of boot camp the Marine Corp is like a regular job. During the day we were in class but at night we partied. Then on the weekends we would rent hotel rooms just to get away from base.

Most of the guys would get prostitutes to keep them company. I personally couldn't imagine paying for an STD. Plus I hung out with pretty boy Reveria so with his good looks and my gift of gab, getting girls to come to our hotel room was no obstacle.

In time I joined the Marine Corp Boxing Team since I thought I was in the best shape that I had ever been in my entire life. The training was very vigorous but I was up for the challenge since I really enjoyed using the speed bag and I had mastered my rope jumping technique. My hands were very quick and I displayed fancy footwork when I spared in the gym. I thought I could beat anybody in my weight class or at least that was my intention.

It was my first fight and I was ready for action. I had the taste for blood just as long as it wasn't mine. The gym looked like the typical boxing ring. Smokey and crowded. Everyone just wanted to see a good fight.

Reveria was my trainer so he was in my corner messaging my shoulders while giving me pointers.

"Alright Papa, this is your big day. Remember everything I told you. Stick and move. Don't be a target.

I was a little nervous seeing so many people.

"Man, this place is packed. I didn't know it was like this."

"Look here Amigo, don't be getting scared on me now. This is fight night, show time. Now get your head in the game and get ready to kick some ass, let's go!"

"I'm cool man, I got this," I tried to sound convincing.

If These Streets Could Talk

My opponent was another Marine who was also from Philly so the crowd was certain that they would see a good fight.

When the bell rang we met in the center of the ring with fury. We both were throwing wild punches lefts, rights, uppercuts, jabs, hooks, trying our best to knock each other out with one punch. The more punches I threw the more tired I got. Each body shot that I received took a percentage of my strength and mine were affecting him too.

Each round lasted three minutes which in the ring seemed like an eternity. I didn't realize how exhausting it was fighting nonstop for just three little minuets.

By the third round my arms felt like they had cinder blocks in them and I think my opponent's did too.

In my corner Reveria was not impressed with my performance.

"Pizarro you look like shit out there. We didn't do all of this training for nothing. You look weak S-A."

Now he started to piss me off.

" Do you want to put on these damn gloves and see what you can do?"

"No."

"Well then shut the fuck up and give me some water."

He gave me a squirt then the bell rang for us to continue.

We both just danced around the ring not throwing any punches looking at each other as if to say, "if you don't hit me, I won't hit you."

Eventually the crowd started booing us and some people even started throwing things into the ring. I mean I really wanted to throw some more punches but my body wouldn't allow me. I was exhausted.

If These Streets Could Talk

Finally the referee just stopped the bout and we both hugged each other and left the ring never to return again. So to all of you boxing fans out there, until you actually try it for yourself, give boxers their props. It's ain't easy and it's not for everyone.

Since the drinking age in North Carolina was eighteen years old, one could easily fall into alcoholism. Every night I was at the E Club drinking and shooting pool. Case had taught me how to shoot pool rather well or at least that was what I thought.

In Philly I was a pretty good pool player but down North Carolina I was just an average Joe. The Marine Corps had guys from all over the United States and they could shoot like pros. Case told me to **never** gamble with anybody whose first name begins with a city like Minnesota Slim or New York Shorty. He said they usually know something and he was right.

This big guy they called Baltimore Reds who packed a mean stick. Red was 6'4", 240 lbs of all muscle. The funny thing about him was he would let you win two or three games straight then would sucker you into betting everything in your pocket on the fourth game and run you off of the table. He would act like it was just luck that he won. He took plenty of my money with that scam until I studied his pattern. Eventually everyone stopped playing him when he got drunk one day and admitted that he shot in professional tournaments back in Baltimore.

Reds and me became pretty tight because he was a hustler and so was I. He also was a good dancer. Whatever the latest dance was at the time we would learn it, master it, and then take it to the club and show off. People in Jacksonville thought we were the coolest guys around with our smooth moves and fly clothes. Occasionally we would have to kick a butt or two of some jealous guys wanting to challenge us because of their lack of dancing skills. Between Big Reds, Pretty Boy Revera, and myself, our knockout record was flawless.

As time went on my drinking started to take its toll. I would constantly get into bar fights. I started failing test and falling behind in automotive class. After the weekends I would come back to formation with my civilian clothes on sometimes still drunk and hung over instead of in my uniform. I would receive article 15's. That's where they took your money or stripes for disobeying orders. It's Uncle Sam's way of punishing you. I was also AWOL (absent without leave) so many times that my family and friends in Philly would question weather or not I was really in the Service.

After a while I got tired of articles 15's so Reds came up with this idea of robbing prostitutes. I thought that he meant snatching their pocketbooks but he had something else in mind.

That weekend me and Reds rented a motel room at this dump out in downtown Jacksonville. Reds assured me that we were going to get paid.

"Ok Pizarro, just bring the hooker up to the room and I'll do the rest."

I went out to the streets and sure enough this skinny, bucktooth; red wig wearing lady approached me.

"Do you need a date baby?"

I was smoking a cigarette.

"Yea, sure, how much?"

"$50 and you got to wear a rubber."

"Alright come on."

I grabbed her by the hand and led the way back to my hotel room.

The entire time we were walking she was talking trash.

"I don't usually do this but I lost my job a few months ago and my rent is $2,100 a month. I use to work for the government too as a secretary but I got laid off talkin about they found cocaine in my piss. I been stopped snorting coke. Plus I got a degree in science that I can't do shit with so I stay high so I don't get mad, you know what I mean baby?" she said laughing as if she was high while telling me this bullshit. All I was thinking was, "I wish she would just shut the fuck up!"

When we got to the hole in the wall of a room she immediately started undressing. I got a good look at her body noticing that she was so skinny I saw her ribs protruding through her skin. Then when I got a good look at her face it was obvious that she had a hard life and was still living it. Her hands were so dry and ashy you could strike a match on them and the veins in her arms bulged out like bodybuilders. I wouldn't pay her $2.00 let alone $50.00 for this bag of bones.

"Here baby, put on this condom," she said throwing the condom on the bed. " And don't try to take it off either. I don't know where yawl nasty Marines been or what ya'll got."

I thought to myself, "You've got to be kidding me, right?"

Just then I saw Reds creeping from out of the bathroom door behind her. He put his index finger up to his lips for me to be quiet.

"BLAM"

He punched her in the back of her head. The prostitute dropped on the floor and was out cold. I couldn't believe it.

"What you standing there looking stupid for, help me search he,." Reds demanded standing over the unconscious hooker.

I opened her purse while Reds patted her down.

"You could have at least warned me that you were going to do some Jessie James punch her in the back of the head shit like that."

"For what. Spontaneous reaction is the best reaction," he said as he pulled a knot of money from out of her bra, put it up to my face, then put it into his pocket.

"Come on, let's get out of here."

I followed Reds out the door looking back at the unconscious prostitute.

After that night Reds and me would go out once or twice a week and victimize prostitutes. We would get a $15 room and bring them up and rob them. Since I always opposed of hitting women, I wasn't feeling good about how we robbed them. Red's on the other hand seemed to enjoy it. I could see the look of pleasure and satisfaction on his face after he knocked them out. I started to believe that he had some kind of sick vendetta against women.

One evening we were on our knockout and rob mission. As usual I would go out and get the prostitute to bring to our room. As Reds was creeping up behind this big country girl that I had picked up from the bar, he stumbled and fell. She immediately turned around and leaped on top of him kicking and scratching him. Reds threw her on the bed, sat on top of her chest and began punching her but she kept on swinging kicking and screaming.

"Knock out bitch, knock out!" he was yelling while he was punching her but Super Ho was not resisting.

I stood there confused. I knew we were supposed to be robbing her but I couldn't imagine me helping Reds beat up a woman. Then Reds started hitting her so hard that blood started coming out of her nose and mouth. I couldn't take seeing anymore so I jumped in.

"Cool out man, you're going to kill her," pushing him from off of her. At that brief moment, she jumped up, pocketbook still in hand, and ran out of the door.

"What the hell is wrong with you Pizarro? Don't you ever grab me when I'm beating a whore down," pointing his finger in my face.

"I thought you were going to kill her man."

" So what if I did. She ain't nothing but a whore."

I looked in Red's eyes and seen that he really meant it. He looked as if he didn't have a problem killing a woman.

"Look man, I don't know what kind of sick abusive past that you might have experienced but I'm not taking no murder rap for your sick demented ass. I get money not bodies."

Reds looked at me and balled up his fist like he was going to charge me when all of a sudden the front door was kicked opened. We both turned around abruptly and seen the bloody prostitute and some little black dude with a Jerry Curl. He was about 5feet tall with a gun in his right hand almost as big as he was pointed at us asking the bloody lady," which one?" "The big one," she said pointing at Reds while holding a bloody handkerchief up to her nose.

He started walking towards Reds with the gun pointed at Red's head and when he got in striking distance he jumped up and hit him with the butt of the gun right between his eyes. Reds went down.

I was a few feet away and wanted to jump him but he pointed the gun at me while he stood over Reds.

"Don't you even think about moving City Boy," he told me with a hard country accent.

He bent down and struck Reds about ten more times with the butt of his gun.

"Don't -you -ever -put -your- hands -on -any -of -my -bitches-again, do you hear me City Boy?"

"Yes, yes sir please don't hit me no more!" Reds cried out with his face full of blood.

If These Streets Could Talk

I wanted to jump Jerry Curl dude but he was too far away and I didn't want to risk getting shot.

He hit Reds a few more times with the gun then when he was satisfied that Reds had enough, he stood up, pointed the gun at me, and headed towards my way indicating that I was next.

I was anxious but I balled my fist up ready for action. The Marine Corp had trained me too well in hand to hand combat to let this little light blue suite wearing, wanna be pimp with a Jerry Curl pistol whip me. Especially after seeing how he just beat Reds like a rented mule, I wasn't having it. He would have to shoot me first.

The prostitute grabbed him by the arm." No Baby not him," still holding the bloody handkerchief up to her nose.

"He saved my life."

He pushed the prostitute towards the door still pointing the barrel of the gun towards me and closed the door. (There goes my angel again).

When they left I ran over to Reds.

"You alright Reds?"

He was lying on the floor in a pool of blood in a fetal position crying like a baby.

"Get off of me," he cried snatching away from my embrace.

"Why didn't you do anything? You could have jumped in and helped me!"

I released my embrace and stood over him.

"I'm sure you saw that the nigga had a gun."

"So what, you could have did something."

While he was still crying I helped him off of the floor. His face and white tee shirt were full of blood.

I escorted him outside where we caught a cab back to our barracks.

If These Streets Could Talk

The entire ride home Reds was holding his bloody t-shirt up to his face crying. I knew that he was in pain but it was pretty annoying listening to a 240 lb. crybaby who liked to beat up on women whimpering all of the way home, even though his face was a mess looking like a soup sandwich.

Both of his eyes were swollen shut so when we got out of the cab I had to guide him by his arm back to our barracks. Deep down inside I was laughing to myself.

"Now he knows how it feels," I thought.

Back on base I explained to the fire watch on duty that we had got into a fight out in town then I got Reds a bag of ice and helped him to his bunk. When Reds finally cried himself to sleep with his face packed with ice, I went to the E Club and shot a game of pool.

In time I got sick of Uncle Sam telling me what to do. Plus I was really missing Yalanna and constantly thinking about how Case and Jones were getting rich off of the drug game while I was making peanuts in the military. That's when I made up my mind to come up with a conniving scheme to get out of the corp. "How could I get out of the Marine Corps before my time served without getting a dishonorable discharge?" I thought long and hard for days then it hit me.

I had recalled that during my physical examination to enter into the Corps that a Navy doctor had told me that I have a mild case of scoliosis, which is just a curvature of the spine, and mine was very mild but I decided to try and run away with it.

From that day forwards my back was killing me. Every time we did PT (physical training) my back hurt. Every time we marched, my back hurt. I should have won a Grammy the way I would go to sick bay bent over in what appeared to be excruciating pain. I even faked falling out a few times during our daily runs to make my plan more realistic.

If These Streets Could Talk

The doctors gave me several test and medication but couldn't find anything except that my spine had a slight curve in it. I found out in time that even with modern day medicine and technology they still haven't come up with a sure back ailment detection.

Finally they shipped me to the casual barracks. That's where they keep all of the Marines pending discharges of all types from medical, to bad conduct, to dishonorable. You stay there until your paper work is finished and your discharge is ready.

We were in the Marine Corp's eyes a bunch of losers, which I didn't care what they thought of me, I just wanted out.

About two weeks before my discharge date I was called down to our investigations unit to talk to this civilian detective. My first thought was he was going to bust me for robbing prostitutes so I mentally prepared myself getting my lie in perfect order but this was a totally different investigation.

When I got to his office he had me confirm that I was private Pizarro and asked me to have a seat. He was a frail looking middle age white guy with a thick mustache and bushy eyebrows. His suit was so tight you could see his heart beat through the jacket and his out of shape weak looking body let me know he wasn't a Marine. He tried to have an aggressive approach but I know a phony when I see one.

When I sat down he handed me a piece of paper.

"Alright Pizarro. I want you to sign the name 'Deborah Collins' on this paper," spelling her first and last name for me as I wrote.

He took the paper that I signed, looked at my Deborah Collins signature suspiciously comparing it to another piece of paper he was holding then he handed them both to me.

When I looked at the two pieces of paper my heart dropped. It was a copy of a check for the amount of $7,300 with what appeared to be my exact handwriting. The signatures were identical. I don't mean close, I mean precise. I always thought that I had horrible handwriting but I must have a twin out there somewhere who has the some atrocious handwriting like me.

He snatched both pieces of paper from my hand.

"OK Pizarro, let's cut through the chase and not waste each others time. You just sign this confession form and I'll assure you that we'll be lenient on you," throwing a confession letter and ink pen across the table at me.

Looking at him like he was stupid, "Sir, with all due respect, I'm not signing shit. I don't know whose signature that is but it sure as hell ain't mine."

"Look Pizarro, even Stevie Wonder can see that that's your handwriting so stop freaking lying and come clean!" he yelled slamming his fist down on the desk.

This guy obviously didn't know who he was dealing with. Like I was supposed to crack under his non-intimidating pressure. I wanted to slap him in his mouth for his little Stevie Wonder joke but I composed myself. Case always told me unless someone actually catches you in doing something to never confess, especially to something that you didn't do.

Detective Dummy got frustrated

"Get out of my office but don't leave the base for the next 48 hours! I'm going to make you come clean if it's the last thing I do. I'll be seeing you again real soon"

When I left his office I was furious but also afraid. I was furious because he tried to make me confess to a crime that I hadn't committed, and I was afraid because the handwriting was so accurate that I almost believed that the signature was mine. I was in total disbelief. Out of all of the bad things that I did and got away with they were actually going to stick me with something that I didn't do but no matter what I wasn't breaking.

The following day Detective Dummy had me in his office all day taking several different hand writing tests. He made me write the alphabet left and right handed which was very difficult to do. I had to print it then write it in cursive left and right handed. Then I had to write Deborah Collins name every way that he could think of. I just casually followed all of his instructions on what he wanted me to do then after about six hours of Sesame Street he got a little aggravated slamming his fist on the desk.

"Dam it Private Pizarro, just stop! You may as well come clean. We know and you know that you forged this freaking check so stop wasting both of our time and sign the damned confession!"

I looked at him and envisioned me grabbing his little grape shaped head and snapping his neck like a rag doll but instead I remained calm. Case always taught me to maintain a certain amount of self control at all times.

I politely said, " You may as well keep the test coming because I'm not confessing to something that I did not do."

Once again he threw me out of his office and told me not to leave the base.

Two weeks had passed and my discharge came through but instead of a medical discharge they gave me a BCD and that doesn't stand for big chicken dinner. It was a Bad Conduct Discharge. I never heard from Detective Dummy again so I assumed he had something to do with the changing of my discharge. That $7,300 check could have landed me 1-3 years in the brig (military prison) for forgery but instead they gave me a Bad Conduct Discharge since they couldn't prove that it was my handwriting. They also assured me that I couldn't get a job at Mc Donald's with a BCD.

If These Streets Could Talk

Out of my four-year contract with Uncle Sam I only served 2½. I really appreciated everything the Marine Corp taught me as far as self-discipline, self-pride, self-respect, and honoring my country. I met a lot of good men and women from all around the United States who would lay their life down for their country but unfortunately I just wasn't one of them. The military isn't for everyone and in time I realized it certainly wasn't for me. Although I'm sure that some of my roots trace back to Africa and Puerto Rico, I wouldn't want to live anywhere but the good old U.S.A.

If These Streets Could Talk

Ch 11 The Introduction

In 1986, when I came home from the Corps I wanted everything that Uncle Sam owed me. I got my G.I. money not thinking that one day I might want to buy a house. I got my education money not thinking that maybe one day I might want to go to college. Yalanna's aunt got me a job at a warehouse so I could have a steady income, and K.K. let me move in to third floor apartment while she and my sisters lived on the second floor. Case, Rochelle, and my newborn nephew Cashes Jr. who they had while I was away lived on the first floor.

Meanwhile the neighborhood seemed a little different. Everything seemed to be going a lot faster than when I left. People were selling anything on the streets. VCRs, TVs, clothes, baby formula, pampers; anything to get a buck. This was the beginning of the crack age. Most people weren't sniffing cocaine anymore they were smoking it. It was the worst thing to happen to people especially people in the hood.

Those that smoked coke didn't realize it, but they were chemists to turn powder cocaine into a solid form. I learned from watching Case and my younger sister Maria cook up some cocaine in his kitchen one day.

When they told me that they were going to smoke it I thought it was like smoking a joint but it was no comparison. They used totally different tools and the stuff was highly addictive.

The anticipation on Maria's face was unbelievable

"Case, hurry and cook it up and don't mess it up like you did last time when you put too much baking soda in it." Maria was actually drooling.

"Look girl, I'm a master at this so sit down and shut up. I got this thing down to a science."

I watched as Case carefully sprinkled the white powder onto a playing card and then added a little baking soda to it. Then he bent the playing card with the contents in it and poured it into a soupspoon then added a few drops of water. He reached in his pocket and pulled out a lighter. He lit the lighter under the spoon until the substance started to boil. Once it reached boiling temperature, he took the heat from under the spoon to let it cool down allowing an oily substance to appear. Then Case added a little cold water to make the temperature drop a little more. He bent a hanger back and forth until the tip snapped off and stuck the tip of the hanger into the spoon and started to stir it slowly making sure not to spill a single drop. The oily residue wrapped around and stuck to the hanger tip looking like a small off-white colored rock. His last tool was a razor-blade, which he used to scrape the rocky stuff off of the hanger and then he put a large piece of the rock into his pipe.

I glanced over at Maria. Her mouth was literally watering. Her eyes looked like high beam headlights and I never noticed before but she looked like she was loosing weight.

"How is it Case, is it good?"

Ignoring her, Case put the pipe up to his mouth and just inhaled slowly holding his breath with his hands over his eyes. He lift his head up then exhaled a thin cloud of white smoke out of his mouth. I got a good whiff of the exhaled smoke. It had a very unique and unpleasant smell to it.

When he removed his hands from in front of his eyes, he had a look on his face that I had never seen on him before as if he were a different person. I got a really eerie feeling watching him smoke crack. It made him look like a totally different person.

Maria snatched the pipe out of his hand, threw a piece of rock into the pipe, her hands shaking uncontrollably, and inhaled. When she exhaled there was a sigh of relief on her face. I couldn't believe this was my little sister smoking crack right in front of me and enjoying it.

Maria was twenty years old, and she had a son while I was away in the Marine Corps and was now six months pregnant with another. She dropped out of school in the seventh grade and was on welfare. My nephew's father was in jail which meant she was living off of KK like the rest of us.

Maria handed me the pipe, "Here G, you try it, it's the best," she said with a kind of weird look on her face.

I took the pipe from her, examined it, and wiped the mouthpiece off with the tip of my shirt. Case reached over and put a piece of rock into the pipe, hands shaking.

"Just inhale slowly."

As I put the pipe to my mouth I took another look at how Case and Maria were looking like zombies. I couldn't believe it but they were really crack heads. I handed the pipe back to Case.

"Naw man, I'll pass." (Thank you angel)

" Suit yourself, that's on you." He took the pipe from me and dropped another rock in it. I left the two of them. I didn't like what I was seeing.

Case's weed business started going downhill after he started smoking crack. He would either not be home when somebody wanted to buy some or he would be home with nothing to sell. At first all of his profit would go to his crack habit. Then he started spending his flip money and couldn't buy any more weed to sell. As a result it left him broke. Rochelle got fed up with him after he started selling things from their apartment like the stereo, VCR and all of his clothes. Then there was the big screen TV that he swore to Rochelle someone broke into their apartment and stole. Rochelle eventually packed up and left with my nephew, which made KK put Case out of the apartment since he couldn't afford to pay $200 a month rent. KK made the mistake of letting Maria move in on the first floor after she had her second son. Then a few months later she was pregnant with a third child.

People would constantly knock on Maria's apartment door asking for weed. KK noticed the non-stop traffic coming to buy so that's when she decided to get a little package of her own.

My cousin Maynard was a big time drug dealer down North Philly whose body was as big as his reputation. His intimidating presence carried power like a Clydesdale and he wore a bald head and had a big fist. He called his fists "Louisville Sluggers." He was definitely a no nonsense, don't fuck with type of guy who had a reputation for drugs, guns, and violence. To look in his eyes too long would send a chill down my spine. I knew there were a lot of skeletons in his closet that he was taking to the grave and I didn't want to be one of them. He knew Case and knew the money that could be made on the first floor if the business was handled correctly. That's when KK called him over and he showed her the ropes.

He showed her the difference between $5 and $10 dollar bags and showed her exactly how much to put in each one. He even showed her how to weigh ¼ and ½ ounces and pounds for the money customers.

KK, the name of this game is no shorts. If somebody wants a $5 or $ 10 bag, then they give you $5 or $10. If they want an ounce or a pound, then they better have all of the money not a dollar short. Also trust no one in this game. I've seen people set up their own mother for a few dollars. Now you handle your business the way that you see fit but I don't trust nobody. That's why I have two arms, one on each side of me. I roll by myself and I do my dirt all by my lonely. And remember in this game you don't have no friends. Personally, I don't need none that's why I sing and talk to myself. If somebody sees me fighting a gorilla, then they better help the fuckin gorilla. I help myself. I don't need nobody else. If you need me for anything, just call and I'll be there."

That was all that Maynard said.

After that KK went on a money mission.

Once KK got cutting and bagging the weed down to a science she was unstoppable. Not only did she pick up where Case had left off, she excelled. You see, unlike Case who would smoke up a lot of his profit, KK didn't smoke at all since she had asthma. Plus, she said weed made her paranoid. She just drank in the evenings so everything that she made was strictly profit.

At first it seemed weird watching my own mother bag up and sell weed until she offered to put me on the payroll.

"Giovanni I can't keep up with these customers so you need to stop acting like you're embarrassed about what I'm doing and help me out. I'll pay you $1,000 a week to cut and bag everything up as it comes in."

I figured $1,000 a week on top of my little factory checks sounds like a winner to me.

Maynard would drop the weed off to us and we would get busy. KK would try to pay him money for the drop offs but he wouldn't take any extra money from her. I think he just got off on seeing people doing illegal activities like him.

"We're family. "I'm just happy to see you get on your feet but I can't keep making these drops for you. KK I'll show G my connections and he can make your runs. Weeds not my business, that kind of money is too slow for me." After that Maynard introduced me to his weed connections. First there was Jim Jim from the projects. I didn't like dealing with him because everything he did had to be done at night like he was trying to set me up or something. We only did business with him for a short time then cut him off.

Then there was my Jamaican boy Country. We liked doing business with him because he wasn't selling anything that he wouldn't smoke himself and be satisfied so everything we bought from him was top grade. Everything was cool with Country until one-day country was found out in Fairmont park tied to a tree with his body burnt to a crisp.

Now my main connection was a Korean guy named Chew and his beautiful wife Yen. They owned a grocery store in West Philly. It was in an area we called Little Saigon. There were a lot of Philippines, Chinese, and Koreans in this area so in order to go there you had to know somebody who knew somebody who knew somebody. When they started talking their native language you could get set up at the drop of a hat and not even know it.

Me and Yen would make eye contact when I entered the store. I would walk around and pick up a few items like bread, milk and cheese and go up to the front counter where I would slide Yen an envelope. Written on the envelope would be the amount of money in the envelope and the amount of weed that I wanted to purchase. Yen would reach under the counter and in addition to my groceries she would put three or four pounds of top quality marijuana in my bag while Chew would be stocking the shelves keeping a close look out around the store. None of the other customers knew that a major drug transaction had just taken place right under their noses.

If These Streets Could Talk

KK and me would sit at the table for hours at a time cutting and bagging weed taking turns running back and fourth to the door when someone knocked. Soon so many people were knocking that we couldn't bag up the weed fast enough. That's when we decided to hire Maynard's little brother Clear to come and work for us.

My cousin Clear got his knick name because unlike Maynard he was a high yellow brother whose skin was so light that you could see his blue veins right through his skin as if he were clear. Plus every since his childhood car accident he had somewhat of a mental disorder. He was certified sick. Let's just say his elevator didn't go all the way up.

Clear was the type of guy that you defiantly wanted on your side mostly because of his loyalty. Whenever there was some trouble or drama, you could best believe that Clear was ready to rock and roll. Violence turned him on.

Outside on the "W" all of my friends were selling cocaine and crack on every corner. Jones and his crew were selling on one side of the street while my boy Zack had his crew on the other. It was all of our neighborhood so as long as the mutual respect was there, there was no problem.

I didn't care because all of Jones and Zack's crew smoked weed, which simply enhanced me and KK's business.

Although it was the crack area, no one had any idea how much money me and KK were making from weed. In time 56th& Walnut St. became known as the one stop shop. Everyone bought weed from our building. Professional people, neighborhood people, the old and young. Everyone who smoked. We even had a few white customers coming from the suburbs into the hood purchasing our product on a regular basis. Once I even saw a bus driver stopping his bus in front of our building to run in and out of our building while passengers were still on the bus looking baffled.

Jones and Zack supplied the powder and rock cocaine and if you wanted a drink the bar was on the other corner. Me and KK didn't realize at the time the risks and danger that came along with this new found profitable occupation we had taken on but we were soon fully introduced to the drug game. I don't care how many degrees or awards a person may possess, without common sense, you're lost. The most dangerous person of all is an educated thug. They are the best crooks because they are educated in both worlds. You see street knowledge is like a sixth sense that gives you a mental advantage over those who lack it. On the streets you have to be very swift and cunning since people are constantly trying to scheme and plot to take any and everything that you have. It's almost like a game of chess. It's survival of the fittest. The strong prey on the weak and only the strong survive. Case taught me not to ever be weak so I thought that I had this street thing down pact. But little did I know, I was about to be educated at the **School of Hard Knocks.**

If These Streets Could Talk

Ch 12 Living large

Big Daddy Kane once said, "Who ever said that money can't buy you happiness, is buying the wrong shit," and he was right.

It was the winter of '89' and KK and I were rolling in cash. Our business was bringing in $1,500 on a bad day and $3,500 on a good day and no one ever even knew. They thought we were just some small time mother and son wanna- be drug dealers but little did they know that we were stinging the streets.

Me and KK would take turns vacationing to different cities, states, and islands just to get away every once in a while just because we could. There's nothing like taking a trip at the drop of a hat and we did it on a regular basis. Atlanta, LA, New York, Bahamas, Cancun. The list goes on and on. You name it we've been there.

Yalanna and I had just gotten back from Las Vegas for a short three-day trip. I had won about $9,000 on the black jack table. I added a few thousand to it and went to the auction and paid cash for a 1988 Murker XR4TI. Not too many people had them. I think Ford teamed up with the Germans to make this vehicle. Mine was black with gray leather interior, heated seats, sunroof, and a turbo kit that allowed me to go from 0 to 60 in 4.5 seconds. I added some chrome rims and an Alpine system to enhance its sound and beauty.

At the time I owned three other cars but my XR4TI was my baby. It was a complete eye catcher. At every stoplight I would get waves and winks from cuties wanting to just sit on my butter leather seats. My player status reached a new high and my phone book runneth over. That XR4TI was a complete girl magnet. It became a job just keeping up with all of the young ladies in my life. Even though I was still with Yalanna, I was also with Kim, Sandy, Dana and Patrice, who all thought they were my main girl and who were all selling my weed for me at their jobs. I was living the best of both worlds.

It was the year 1990 during the middle of the summer, and I was driving down 56th St. when I saw about ten or fifteen guys standing around in a circle. In the hood that only means a few things. Either there was a fight of some sort or it was a crap game.

I pulled over, and after I realized I recognized mostly everybody in the crowd, I got out to join the festivities. I was fresh to death wearing all white.

I pushed my way to the front of the crowd to see what the number was and who was shooting the dice so I could place a bet. When I looked down, low and behold it was no other than Zack on his knees sweating like a Hebrew slave. And standing over him was Shank betting against him. I watched as poor Zack threw craps on every roll crapping out every time loosing all of his money. I yelled out to him, "Zack, what you doin on your knees dude?" He just looked up at me and kept shooting.

"G, they got me down $6,000 and I'm not getting off these dice until I gets mines back."

Shank smiled while counting his winnings.

"That's right Big Boy. Just keep shooting those dice, you're doing just fine," he said to Zack licking his thumb while counting his money. Shank saying that really pissed me off since I knew he was just showing off for the crowd of younger guys. I also couldn't believe everybody was betting against Zack and he was loosing every time. I had to do something.

When Zack threw craps again I butted in.

"Yo Zack, let me holler at you for a minute."

One of Shank's lynching men got upset about me stopping the game. "Hold up. How the fuck you gonna just jump in the middle of the game and stop the flow? I got a lot of money out here. I think you better step off."

I looked at him as if he was kidding.

"Pump your breaks young boy. This here is grown folks business so don't get it twisted," I said lifting up the front my T-shirt exposing my 9mm Glock.

Shank butted in.

"Cool that shit out G. We're having a good time over here and don't need no dumb shit ," he said pulling up the front of his shirt exposing the silver .45 caliber he had in the front of his pants showing he wasn't intimidated. Then he directed his attention to his boy.

"Chill the fuck out and let them talk for a minute. He probably wants to give him some lessons." The small crowd started laughing as I pulled Zack away from the crowd.

When I pulled Zack to the side I reached up and put both of my hands on both of his shoulders and looked him dead in his eyes.

"Look man, me and you have been down this road before so don't choke on me now. Case taught both of us how to hit every number on those dice and I'd be damned if I'm going to watch you let Shank and those little nuts walk away with your cash."

I reached in my pocket and counted out five one hundred dollar bills and put them on his hand.

"Now I'm betting with you so go back over there and get your money back from those motherfuckers."

Zack shook my hand while at the same time hugging me.

"Your right G man. Let's serve these faggots."

People I tell you no lie. Zack got back on his knees and hit every number on the dice while the whole time I was cheering him on like a Philadelphia Eagles cheerleader while winning with him.

"Yo Zack, hit that damn six so I can put that new system in my car." Zack shook the dice and threw them. "And while you're at it, put in some new speakers too. Six!" he yelled while throwing two threes right back.

Shank and the entire crowd were pissed. Shank even reached down for the dice.

"Let me see those dice Zack."

Shank examined them then handed them back to Zack.

"G, I know yaw ain't throw no fuckin hooks in the game," Shank looked over at me suspiciously.

"Are you loosing that much that you have to accuse us of throwing crooked dice in the game? Man stop bitchin and let Zack shoot the dice," I said as I counted my money.

Zack continued to hit numbers while I bet everybody in the circle sending them home one by one broke.

In less than one hour me and Zack won everybody's money. You'd be surprised how much money is involved in some street games. That's why you have to know the people you're shooting against since a crap game can go sour at any time. I've seen people stabbed, shot or beat down severely from someone trying to cheat or just a plain sore looser wanting his money back. Believe me, that was one crap game the whole neighborhood never forgot.

If These Streets Could Talk

Ch 13 Let's Party

My closest friends consisted of about ten guys and fifteen girls and believe me we were tight. When we greeted each other the guys would shake hands and hug while the girls would greet us with a kiss on the cheek. We were like family.

The majority of my crew had Arabic knick names claiming to be Muslim and needless to say eating pork was forbidden in our gang even though most of us were raised eating it.

Also if somebody had a problem with one of us, then they had a problem with all of us. One phone call from someone in danger or distress would bring us together like Jerico's Army.

Aside from being drug dealers, thieves, and con artists, my friends and I were party animals. It became a ritual that every Friday and Saturday night me, Jones, Zack, and the rest of our squad would get together to go to the club. Everyone would try to out fashion one another to see who could wear the flyest gear. The girls would rock their leather mini skirts, big gold earrings and fur jackets while the guys wore printed Versace shirts and alligator boots.

After seeing Biggie Smalls in a video, I went out and bought some Pink alligator boots, a hand made gray silk double breasted suit, and a pink silk shirt. I figured hey, if Biggie could rock pink, so could I. You see, in the early 90's to wear pink you had to really have confidence in your masculinity. When I first wore my pink alligator boots Jones said I looked like the tooth fairy, but when I stepped in the club and took off my white cashmere coat and white beaver Bosalini hat, the girls knew that I was a major figure. Only a real player could wear pink boots and get away with it.

If These Streets Could Talk

The Heavy Hitters Night club on 59th & Market St. in West Philly was the drug dealer's playground. It was ghetto fabulous. Everybody who was anybody would party there. Even though the 60th St. crew dominated The Heavy Hitters, the "W" made our presence known by throwing money around with our expensive clothes and jewelry, buying $100 bottles of champagne by the case.

The Heavy Hitters Night Club had three bars located through the club. The entire center of the club was a very spacious dance floor and the DJ was a master of , continuously cutting and scratching. There was a stage for those of us who wanted to be seen or look at ourselves while we danced that was enclosed by mirrors. The waitresses were very attractive and well built. They had no problem running nonstop, serving drinks and food because the tips were very satisfying. We would drink, dance, and laugh all night long without any worries or trouble.

Occasionally, I would wake up the next morning with a complete stranger that I had picked up from the club. If I liked her I would take her to breakfast, give her a few dollars to fix her hair, then move onto the next one. It sounds callous but that was the way it was. Money, respect and power ruled.

Case taught me that if you want to launch big ships you have to go where the water is deep. On one of our Saturday night binges, me, Zack and Jones decided to check out this new spot we had heard about down Center City called The Phoenix. In time we had either dealt with or slept with the finest that the Heavy Hitters had to offer and it started to bore us so we decided that it was time to expand our horizons and we couldn't have picked a better spot. The Phoenix was infested with big legs, mini skirts, and small waists from all over. Delaware, NJ, NY, and Philly's finest. Our mouths watered at the sight of fresh meat and we couldn't wait to sink our teeth in. Wearing our Saturday night finest, we knew exactly how to attack.

There was a long line of people waiting to get into the club so the three of us walked up to the front of the line. I pulled a fifty-dollar bill out of my pocket and held it in front of the bouncer's face.

"We have reservations," I said waving the money in the air. He moved the divider to let the three of us in front of the crowd. "This way gentleman," slipping the money into his shirt pocket. Then some heavy set girl in line started complaining. "How are you going to let them in front of us? I've been in line for a half hour. That's not fair and I want to see the manager!," she demanded. The bouncer turned to her. "What's not fair is what you're doing to that little piece of material you call a skirt, stretching it to its limits. Now turn your fat ass around and mind your damned business before I won't let you in at all."

A few people started laughing as the big girl got out of line and started walking away.

"Fuck this dumb ass club. It ain't the only one in the city. I'll go party somewhere else."

As she walked away you could see her butt was shaking from side to side in her little skirt. It was plain to see she wasn't wearing any underwear. "Well party somewhere else!," the bouncer yelled. "Damn. Would you look at that. Doesn't that look like a water bed without the frame?" I heard everybody in line laughing the as three of us walked into the club.

Inside Zack took control of the bar dropping a fifty dollar bill on the barmaid. "Make sure that me and my boys thirst stays quenched, we don't like lines," Zack said sliding the barmaid the $50 bill pointing to me and Jones making sure the barmaid knew who to cater to. "No problem big boy," she said as she slid the money into her bra. Then a young lady who knew Zack seemed so excited to see him she just yelled out, "Hey Zack, what's up baby?"Zack turned towards her with a disgusted look on his face.

"Damn! Everywhere I go, there's a ho that I know!"
The young lady looked in disbelief as me and Jones laughed at her. "Why did you play her like that Zack, you know you're a big boy around here."

Zack was a big boy too. At 6'3 and 230 lbs, he possessed power in his presence. Most of his victims said he possessed power in his punches. He was my kind of guy. A one punch knock out artist.

In the club we made our way to the pool tables pretending to shoot for $100 a game. A crowd of women surrounded our table to check out the battle but little did they know that after we left the club, we would give each other our money back. It was just a clever ploy to lure woman over to us.

After a few drinks and dances me and Zack stood up on the balcony casing the place out looking for our next victims while Jones was dancing with two fine young ladies. This is what we did, we were players. As me and Zack looked down from the balcony, in came two half shirt, mini skirt wearing, tight body having, hoochie mammas. Zack spotted them first.

"Yo G let's attack," he said pulling at my shirt sleeve, pointing at the girls. I looked down.

"Naw man they ain't shit," I said while sipping my drink.

"Man how do you know they ain't shit from here?"

"Because I'm from the ghetto and I know rats when I see them."

He laughed, "Whatever man. I'm from the ghetto too, and I know a freak when I see one and my freak detector is going haywire." He headed towards the staircase. "Go ahead man," I took another sip. "Get um killer!"

"Just be careful. Remember the last time your freak alarm went off you almost slept with a transvestite."

I started laughing while throwing playful punches at Zack. He didn't like it. He started walking back towards me.

"Damn G," with a disgusted look on his face. " I thought we weren't going to bring that shit up anymore."

Cool out dude, I'm just messin' with you man. Here, handing him a breath mint. He refused it.

" I don't need no mint, I got chewing gum."

"That's my point. Get rid of the gum. Players never chew."

He reluctantly took the mint and put it in his mouth.

"I'm going to hit the dance floor," I said as I slammed down the rest of my drink and sat the empty glass on the balcony ledge.

When you're out clubbing the only difference between a pretty girl and an ugly girl is a fifth of liquor. I danced a few more times, got a few more phone numbers from girls and then about ten shots of Southern Comforts later, the little hood rat in the mini skirt that me and Zack had seen earlier from the balcony started to look like Janet Jackson.

With my blurred vision and slurred speech I approached her.

"So what's your name Shorty?," I stood behind her looking her up and down from the back. When she turned around I caught her eyes lock onto my diamond, hand crafted necklace.

"My name is Marnissa but they call me Nis."

I watched her eyes give me the head to toe once over.

"All right Nis, can I get a kiss?" I asked leaning forward to kiss her on the cheek. I couldn't believe she actually let me. (First indication of a hood rat. Didn't even know my name and let me kiss her. Just plain **nasty**.)

"So Miss Nis, can I offer you a ride home?"

She appeared to think for a second.

"Thanks but no thanks. I'm staying with my cousin and my aunt trips out when we get rides home from guys."

"All right then, suit yourself but let me at least buy you a drink." "Ok, that's cool."

I grabbed her hand leading her towards the bar. I thought to myself, "I got this one." I also tried not to stagger while I was walking since the eleventh shot of Southern Comfort was banging me in the head really hard.

It was around 2:00 am and the club was closing. Zack walked up to me with his arm around a six foot tall model looking female with a tight red dress and a head full of weave down to her butt looking like a fake Tyra Banks.

Giving me his sinister looking smile, Zack said,

"G, me and my new found friend are going to breakfast. I'll call you in the morning." I grabbed his arm pulling him close enough to whisper in his ear.

" Make sure that she doesn't have testicles." He snatched away from my grip as I laughed at him watching him walk away obviously not fond of my remark. He gave me the middle finger as they exited the club.

Jones was walking toward the exit with the two girls he was on the dance floor with his hands around both of their waist.

"Come on G, let's ride out," he yelled as they walked out the door.

"Is that what they call you, G," Nis asked.

"Yeah that's what they call me."

"Well G, it looks like you have entertainment for the evening," pointing at Jones walking out the door with the two females.

"Oh no baby it's not like that, those are my cousins."

She laughed at my lie while writing her phone number down on a napkin.

"Well anyway here's my number so just call me Maybe we can hang out sometime."

I looked down at the napkin.

"A 610 area code. Where do you live?"

" I live in Coatesville but don't worry, it'll be worth the trip."

She slid her hand down the front of my chest and stomach stopping at my waistline.

I watched her as she walked away. She was short and stacked. Her calf muscles were so tight they looked like cigarette boxes with strong stallion thighs to match. She had a small waist with breast the size of oranges and a cute face just the way I like it.

"Yeah, "I thought", I will be seeing Miss Nis again real soon."

When I woke up the next morning I didn't know where I was. I was in a bed at the Embassy Suites hotel lying next to one of the girls that me and Jones had brought home from the club. I immediately reached for my pants to make sure my money was still in my pockets. Jones and his girlfriend were comatose on the other bed right beside us.

I looked down and was relieved to see a used condom on the floor next to my bed. I couldn't recall in detail what happened last night but at least I did use a condom. Intoxicated or not condoms were my friend.

My unknown friend woke up from me moving around in the bed. With her weave and makeup totally out of order.

"Good morning G," rubbing her hands down my back.

I impolitely jerked away from her touch.

"Who you?" I blurted out rudely. She sat up in the bed.

"What the hell do you mean who am I? You knew exactly who I was last night when you were in between my legs."

I slipped my pants on.

"Well I don't know you now."

I pulled a $20 bill from out of my pants pocket.

"Here, go catch a cab, it's been real."

She stood up on the bed with her hands on her hips exposing her nakedness.

"Who do you think you are treating me like some cheap ho talking about it's been real? You ain't all that you big head bastard."

"That's all right because my pockets are big too."

She pointed down at my genital area.

" Yea well that's **all** that's big."

Her trying to insult my manhood pissed me off.

"Look here porno girl, why don't you go to the Wizard of Oz and try to get some self respect because you're NASTY! You can't disrespect me because you don't even respect yourself. You just see a nice car and some fly gear and assume that you can be a part of my world. I don't think so! You're just another episode in this soap opera of my life. Now wake up your brain dead girlfriend and get the hell out of here before I start blasting!"

I lifted up my shirt to expose my 9-millimeter.

Shaking her girl friend frantically and picking up the $20 from off of the floor that I gave her for cab fare.

"Come on Shaketa, wake up! These niggas ain't about shit."

Just then Jones popped up.

"Yo G what you doin man?" he said while wiping the sleep from his eyes. "I wanted to hit that one more time." "Well your boy just messed it up for you because you ain't hitten shit!" Porno Girl yelled.

She and her girl slipped on their clothes and headed toward the door.

" I hate ya'll fake-ass drug dealers," she said as she slammed the door.

I just stuck out my tongue at her like a little kid.

"Jones, didn't I tell you about setting me up when I'm drinking Southern Comfort. I could have slipped up and sexed that chicken head without using a rubber."

Lifting up his covers and looking around his bed.

"Oh no!" .

"What's wrong?"

I asked him with concern.

"Don't tell me she stole your money."

"No man even worse. I think I did sex her without a rubber." I thought to myself that it wasn't the first time and wouldn't be the last.

The following week was Jones' birthday so he decided to throw himself a birthday bash at the Heavy Hitters. The entire "W" was present dressed in our Saturday night best having a ball.

I was chillin in the VIP booth when I noticed from a distance Shank walking in the club with who other than Sweets. She was holding on to his arm with two of his thug buddies tagging close behind them. Sweets was wearing a $1,200 denim Mochimo outfit. I knew the price because I had bought the same outfit for Yalanna. Shank must have given the bouncer a heavy tip because Sweets was only eighteen years old and didn't have any I.D. to get into the club.

I didn't want to seem like I was upset seeing her at the club with Shank but deep down inside I was furious. I always told her to stay away from Shank because he was trouble. You see, Shank had a crack house on Ruby Street that was pulling in major cash and his head was bigger than his pockets. You couldn't tell him he wasn't Tony Montana or somebody.

Shank walked up to my VIP booth pulling Sweets close behind him.

"Well look at G in the VIP," exposing his bucked teeth. I tried to keep my cool.

"What's up Shank? Hey Sweets," I said with a fake grin. Sweets looked totally embarrassed.

"Hey G," Shank asked, " you don't mind if we sit with you for a few do you?"

"Well I got some of my peeps comin but I guess ya"ll can squat for a few," knowing I didn't really want him sitting with me.

Then one of Shank's boys interrupted.

"That's alright Shank. I reserved a booth over here for us."

Shank immediately headed his way.

"Now that's what I'm talking about! All right G we're out. Oh! By the way, do you have any weed on you?"

Smiling that little bucktooth smile of his.

" I might need a nickel bag or two for later."

It took all of my composure to refrain from jumping across the table and choking him. "Naw man. When I'm out partying, I'm out partying. I don't mix business with pleasure. Why, do you have any powder on you?" I asked him in retaliation.

He lift his arm in the air showing me the personalized handcrafted bracelet that was around his wrist.

"It should be obvious by my bracelet alone that I don't push nicks and dimes. Unlike you, I push weight."

At that comment the blood shot straight to my head and I couldn't hold it in anymore so I jumped up out of my seat.

"Well I'm about to push my foot… "just then Jones came out of nowhere interrupting holding a bottle of Don Per ion .

"Shank, G, can a brother get a birthday toast from his boys or what?"

Both Shank and me took a champaign glass from Jones while we eyed each other down. Inside my heart I knew it wasn't over and so did he. It just wasn't the time or place.

As the evening went on it pissed me off looking over at Shank's table watching him and his boys sitting at the table playing Pitty Pat. They were actually gambling at the club in the VIP section. What a nut, and Sweets was just sitting there with him drinking champagne. I was pissed.

I walked over to Shank's table.

"What yaw playin, Pat?"

Shank had a big cigar in the side of his mouth.

"That's right young boy, $100 a hand, you want in?"

"I actually just wanted to show you a card trick."

Shank's fake ass bodyguard stepped in front of me, "Beat it little man!"

"Naw, wait. Let's see what kind of trick Houdini got under his sleeve." Shank handed me the deck of cards. "Go ahead, entertain me."

I started shuffling the cards as I looked over at Sweets. She gave the please don't do it since she seen me do this trick plenty of times before. I spread the deck out like a fan in my hands with the numbers facing Shank.

"Ok Shank, pick a card, any card, as long as it's a card but don't let me see it."

Damn G, you stopped my card game for this elementary shit! This is the oldest trick in the world."

"Trust me, you never seen this trick before, I just learned it.

Shank pointed at the card so Sweets and his boys could see it.

"Ok you got it?"

"Yea I got it. Hurry up with this corny ass trick so I can finish gambling."

I shuffled the card thoroughly. I then looked at the cards, then at Shank, then the cards, then back at Shank. Then I went into my psychic mode. I put my hand on my forehead and closed my eyes like I was in deep concentration. Then I pulled a card out of the deck and put it on the floor in front of Shank's foot. "That's your card right there." Shank's flunky went to pick up the card when Shank grabbed his shoulder stopping him.

"Hold up G. Your telling me that you just picked the card I pointed to?"

"That's right genius. That's your card right on the floor in front of you."

Shank reached in his pocket pulling out a knot of money, I bet you $500 that's not my card."

I also pulled out five one hundred dollar bills, "it's a bet."

Shank turned to Sweets and his boys, "ya'll hear this right?' Everyone agreed that they heard the bet. Shank bent down to pick up the card and as soon as his hand touched the card that was on the ground I took the rest of the fifty one cards that I was holding, raised my hand high in the air and bust Shank in the head with the deck of cards ricocheting off of his head flying everywhere. Sweets, Shank's crew, and everybody in the immediate area burst out laughing at Shank as he was still on one knee rubbing the top of his head. I dropped my five, one hundred dollar bills on the floor in front of Shank.

"Dam, that's not your card."

I received hi fives from people as I walked away. One Dude gave me $100 and said, "Man I got to use that trick. Needless to say it was worth five hundred dollars to humiliate Shank like I did.

Near the end of the evening me and Sweets ran into each other coming out of the bathroom at the same time. I pulled her to the side.

"Why in the hell are you here with Shank? You know I don't like or trust his ass. Are you crazy or just plain stupid?"

She rubbed her hand across my back trying to calm me down.

"I know G don't trip. He asked me to go out with him and when I told him that I didn't have anything to wear he said that he'd buy me something. I just played him for this Michino outfit, you like?"

She slowly spun around for me to give her the once over. Looking her up and down, I said "Yeah I likes but look, Shank don't give nobody nothing for free. After the club tonight he's going to be looking for some payback."

"Well I told Shank from the door that nothing will be going down tonight." Rubbing her baby soft hands across my face, "Chill out G. I got this thing under control. You know you taught me well. Now let me get back to the table before he comes looking for me."

She gave me a kiss on the cheek and walked away. I watched Sweets and Shank on the dance floor as he fed her drinks while rubbing all over her body. I thought to myself how much I really care about Sweets but sometimes people have to learn for themselves. Experience is the best teacher.

All of a sudden the music stopped and a heavy set lady with a full length fur coat stood in the middle of the dance floor holding a police badge in the air.

"Alright everybody out! This club is officially closed due to under aged drinking." She had about ten or fifteen uniform cops with her pushing people towards the exit. Me, Jones and Zack grabbed a few bottles of liquor from behind the bar on our way out and stuffed them under our coats while people were running, yelling, cursing, and screaming all of the way out the door.

If These Streets Could Talk

After all of the excitement we all met up outside in the parking lot and planned to gather back on the W to keep the party going.

While everybody was talking and complaining about what had just taken place I was looking all through the crowd but I didn't see Sweets anywhere but I did see her girlfriend Ashley.
"Hey Ash, when you see Sweets tell her the everybody is meeting on the "W" for some drinks"

"Alright G, I'll tell her when I see her."

I drove out of the parking lot still trying to spot Sweets. Her being with Shank still wasn't sitting well with me. Plus there was no telling what kind of stolen car he was driving.

All of my friends followed me in their cars back to the "W" where KK was already having a party down the basement of our building for her and her friends. She agreed to let us join the party as long as we contributed our stolen booze.

We had a ball partying with the old heads trying to do The Bop. I've got to admit, The Bop has got to be one of the smoothest dances ever invented especially when you have two people who master all of the steps.

We ate, drank and danced the night away just like old times. Yalanna had a little too much to drink and vomited in the middle of the dance floor. KK didn't even get upset. She just had somebody clean it up and the party went on. I carried Yalanna up to my apartment, carefully took off her clothes, and laid her down. As I went back downstairs to the party I thought to myself, "Damn life is good."

I was into a deep REM sleep when my telephone rang at 6:05 am and since the party ended around 5:00 am that meant I was only asleep for 55 minutes. Yalanna was still out cold with a hangover and didn't hear the phone ring. With my gravel, hangover voice I answered, "Hello?"

It was Sweets. She was crying hysterically saying something that I couldn't understand. "Sweets it's 6:00 in the morning, slow down so I can understand you".

She cried, "Shank raped me!"

I was suddenly wide-awake like someone threw a bucket of ice cold water in my face. I felt my heart drop in my chest. I was numb. She continued, "He took me to the hotel saying that his boy was having an after party there. I told him I didn't want to go since Ashley told me that you said to meet you on the 'W' I was a little drunk, but I knew something was wrong because when we got there the room was totally dark. G, he pushed me on the bed and tried to kiss me. I kept saying no then he slapped me and tore my shirt off. I tried to fight but he was too strong. Then he literally ripped my jeans off. G, he raped me, he raped me…."

Her crying through the phone made me want to reach out and embrace her. Those words tore through my soul with a fury. My head felt like it was going to explode as I felt nauseous picturing the scene. Sweets kept talking but I didn't know what else she was saying at that point. The only thing that was on my mind was to kill Shank.

I was slipping my clothes on while she was talking trying not to wake up Yalanna. I reached in between my mattress and pulled out my 9-millimeter checking the clip assuring that it was fully loaded. I tried to calm her down.

"Sweets you have to try to pull yourself together Baby. I'll take care of Shank." "G, don't do anything stupid. Shank is a jerk and he's going to get his."

"Sweets I got to go, I'll call you back in a few."

"Wait G wait!"

I hung up the phone, threw on my black leather hat and jacket, and stuffed my 9 mm between my jeans and the small of my back. Yalanna woke up eyes red and her hair wild with an obvious hangover.

"Where are you going Baby?"

"I've got to make a pick up, I'll be right back."

"Ok, bring back some breakfast," she said as she just dropped back off to sleep. I kissed her forehead and headed out the door.

Shank must have wanted to go to war with me. He knew how I felt about Sweets. Him raping her was like him raping me. This was going to be more than retaliation. This was his death wish. I jumped in my car and peeled off.

On the way to Shank's house all I thought about was him violating Sweets. I convinced myself I didn't care if his boys were outside I was taking him down. And if anyone got in my way, they could get it to.

As I approached Shank's block I took out my 9 and pulled the chamber back making sure I was locked and loaded. Case told me never to pull a gun on anyone unless your ready to use it and I was going to use it to its full capacity. My adrenalin level was at its peak and I could hear my heart beating in my chest.

I made a left turn onto Ruby Street with my gun on my lap and stopped suddenly as I saw a bunch of people and police cars surrounding Shanks house. I quickly tucked my gun under my seat as I slowly backed out of the block trying to not draw any attention to myself. I parked my car, put my gun in my glove compartment and walked toward Shank's house.

"Damn," I thought, " Sweets must have called the cops and told them what had happened." From a short distance I could see the police escorting Shank out of his house in handcuffs. All he was wearing were some jeans and a white tee shirt. I walked up close enough so he could see my face. As we caught each other eyes Shank looked at me grinned and said, "Yea, whatever mother fucker!, " as they loaded him in the back of the paddy wagon. I was furious that the police had beat me to Shank. There was no doubt in my mind that his blood would have been shed that day. Little did Shank know that my angel had saved **him** that morning.

If These Streets Could Talk

Ch 14 If It Ain't Rough It Ain't Right

After Shank got sentenced five to ten years in prison for assault, rape, and drug charges after the police raided his house, Sweet's mom sent her to Florida to live with her aunt. It really broke my heart because I never saw or heard from her again. It's funny how a person can have such a major impact on your life and then disappear into thin air. Life's funny like that sometimes.

Back on the "W" Yalanna started getting fed up with me spending so much time selling weed especially since I quit the job that her aunt got me at the factory. I had no other choice since our weed business was going so well it required so much of my time.

Yalanna, on the other hand, was really moving up at her job at the Law office becoming the youngest and only black head paralegal.

" G, I want to move out of the hood. I'm doing really good at my job and I want to live in a better environment. I've been looking at the Korman Suites in Penrose. I think I'll get an apartment out there."

"Anything you want baby. Just tell me what you need."

This was the perfect opportunity for me to get her out of the neighborhood so I could breath a little and be the player that I wanted to be without her living right around the corner.

Yalanna's apartment at Korman Suites was definitely a step up from the neighborhood. It had private parking in front of the building with a stone path leading through the grass to her apartment door. There was an alarm system as you entered the very spacious living room and the chandelier in the dining room was mesmerizing. It had cream wall to wall carpet and her bathroom was very large with a jacuzzi and inside one of the bathroom closets was a washer and dryer.

The bedroom had a walk-in closet and one side of the wall was completely mirrored. Although the apartment was lavish, Yalanna didn't have any furniture. I told KK about her apartment and she insisted that we fully furnish it and we did.

We bought her a white Italian leather sectional complete with sofa, love seat, recliner and ottoman. We also purchased a 52-inch black lacquer surround sound swivel Panasonic color television set, cable ready of course. We also purchased a cherry oak wood king size bedroom set with overhead lights and mirrored background with twin wardrobes.

In her dining room we put a marble dining room table with matching chairs.

When Yalanna came home from work that evening I was at her apartment preparing us a candlelight seafood dinner complete with snow crab legs, shrimp, steamed muscles, scallops and lobster tails. I also steamed some garlic broccoli. (I forgot to mention that a brother could cook)?

When she walked in the door she started hyperventilating. I ran over to her because I thought she was having a heart attack. "Breathe baby breathe," I said rubbing her back. When she finally calmed down she started screaming and jumping up and down. "Thank you G thank you, you are the bomb!" she said kissing and hugging me so hard that she nearly broke my neck.

" Well you know I try to do what I can do when I can do it," I replied boastfully.

I always get pleasure in making Yalanna happy because she appreciates anything that I do for her from buying her a bag of potato chips to a long walk and talk on the beach. Knowing that she was set up out Penn Rose eased my conscious a little for all of the times she hung in there with me through the good and the bad. Now, let the games begin.

First I called Marnissa. I couldn't stop thinking about that little athletically built body of hers. When Marnissa told me that she lived in Coatesville I didn't know it looked so rundown. Then to make matters worse I didn't bring my 9mm because I didn't want to risk getting jammed up out of town. Without my gun I felt like an infant without a diaper, butt naked.

Coatesville to me looked like a big North Philly (no disrespect to North). The streets were dirty, there was graffiti everywhere, and the people looked poor. I thought again, "damn I should have bought my gun." Marnissa had me meet her at her sister's apartment, which was in the projects. "Damn, I should have bought my gun" When I pulled up in my XR4TI all eyes were on me like I was a movie star or a major league ball player. I wanted to get back in my car and go back home but I would have looked suspect or like a punk and I couldn't have that.

I went to ring the bell looking back at my car like it might be the last time that I would see it in one piece. "Damn, why didn't I bring my gun?" Marnissa opened the door and looked at me with those pretty brown eyes. "Did you have a problem finding the apartment?"

"Naw Baby. I thought I told you that I was a Marine? I could find one of those kids on the back of a milk carton if I put my mind to it." She laughed. "Come inside Silly."

Little did she know my stomach was doing cartwheels inside. "I should have brought my gun." When I stepped inside of the apartment the smell of marijuana smacked me right in the face. The apartment was small but neatly kept. The furniture looked modern but cheap. Three of her girlfriends and two guys were all getting as high as they wanted to be. I saw weed and a half empty bottle of Alize' on the table that they sat around and all of them were holding glasses. She introduced me to everyone. Holding me by the hand, " Hey everybody, this is "G". The girls said, "Hi," but the guys didn't greet me with a handshake. (First sign of player haters. Real men shake hands when they meet).

I ran my eyes around the entire room looking for any signs of foul play making sure that this ghetto cutie wasn't setting me up. I caught one of her girls eyes lock onto my diamond infested Rolex watch while I continued to sense tension from the guys in the room.

One of her girl friends walked up to me and reached for my necklace trying to read the engraving.

"This is nice, does that say Giovanni?"

Nis stepped in grabbing her wrist.

" No it says keep your hands off!"

"You ain't got to get all like that Nis," snatching away from Marnissa's grip. Marnisa grabbed me by the hand.

"Come on G. Lets take a ride to the mall," she said as she rolled her eyes at her over curious girlfriend.

When we walked out the door, I felt a sense of relief to see my car still in one piece. I was also glad to be getting out of the projects but I had to play cool. I couldn't let Marnissa see any signs of me being weak or afraid.

At the mall I took Marnissa on a mini-shopping spree. Although she was a ghetto cutie she was like school in the summer time. No class. I could tell by her choice of stores that her taste was sort of average. The Gap, Learners, and Bare Feet, were her idea of quality clothing.

"Check this out," I told her. "Why don't you let me pick out your clothes and if you don't like my taste then we'll do it your way." She agreed so I led the way.

First I took her to Enzo and picked out a hot pair of knee high Italian leather boots with a three-inch heel and matching purse. Then we swung around to "bebe" since she had a petite build. I got her to try on a leather mini skirt to match the boots and a fitted camel hair blouse to show off her small waist and perky breast. And since no outfit is complete without suitable under garments where else but Vicki hush hush (Victoria's Secret). I picked out one of my favorites, cherry red sheer bra with matching sheer thongs. I even got her a manicure and pedicure to complete her makeover.

I must admit that I changed this little ghetto cutie into a classy beauty. That outfit really gave her the look that I was accustomed to seeing on my woman but one thing I learned quickly. You can take a girl out of the ghetto but you can't take the ghetto out of the girl and it showed at dinner. Her table manners were atrocious. She was smacking and talking with food in her mouth while she was eating and while licking her fingers. She insisted on taking off her boots at the dinner table complaining that they hurt her feet. She even went to the restroom barefoot. It was embarrassing.

Next, not only did she fail to put her dinner napkin on her lap while she ate but she actually took it and blew her nose with it at the table. Then to top it off as we were leaving, she actually doubled back to the table and took five dollars from the twenty five dollar tip that I left for the waiter saying that it was to large a tip.

In spite of everything I was still infatuated by her ghetto beauty so I took her straight to the hotel after dinner.

At the hotel she made me promise that if we spent the night together it would be official that we were boyfriend and girlfriend. Letting my hormones take control and being mesmerized by her athletically built body in those cherry red thongs, I could do nothing but agree.

Slowly but surely I started spending less time with Yalanna and more time with Marnissa. I even allowed Marnissa to step a little closer in my world by letting her ride along with me on some of my weed pick ups. Then on top of that I even showed her how to cut and bag the weed up. I let her in on where my floor safe was located in my apartment and where I kept my guns, money and jewelry.

We were like a ghetto Bonnie and Clyde. I always thought of myself as being pretty clever but Ms. Nis was a step ahead of me and I was blinded. She had my nose wide opened or on the street they would say, "I was whipped."

Marnissa persuaded me to give her some weed to sell over in Coatesville. I would give her weed but she would never give me the money spending it on shopping. Having so much money and being gullible at the same time, I would just give her more and accepted the fact that she was ripping me off.

After awhile Yalanna started getting suspicious about our lack of time together but I didn't care. Like I said, Marnissa had my nose wide open. It was a Saturday night and I was headed to Coatsville to see Marnissa. I had made a pickup earlier that day so I borrowed Zack's dirty 38 for protection, but I forgot to give it back to him so it was under my passenger's seat. I also had half of a fifth of Southern Comfort under the seat and the other half in me. The alcohol had me grooving so I got a little off course and ended up in Chester. I didn't realize my XR4TI was missing a headlight so when I drove past a police car he immediately made a u-turn and put on his lights pulling me over. One. I was shook. Two. I was drunk. Three. I had a half of bottle of Southern Comfort under my seat and Four. I had Zack's dirty . 38 with I don't know how many bodies on it.

As the cop approached my car, I instantly sobered up and my brain went to work. I saw he was a young white guy who looked like he just got out of high school and took the police test. He reached my window. "License and registration."

If These Streets Could Talk

I took out my wallet and slowly reached for my registration in the glove compartment as he shined his light on my every movement. I handed them to him.

"Officer I knew something like this was going to happen." He flashed his light in my eye. I squinted from the beam of light as I continued my story trying not to slur my words. " I'm over here cheating on my fiancé, and I knew something bad was going to happen."

Then he smiled and took the light off my face. "You see, you shouldn't be cheating. Is she a good looking woman?"

"Is she?," I said as I showed him a picture of Yalanna I carry in my wallet.
He examined it. "Yeah she is a cutie."

Just then another police car pulled up across from us. This was an older white haired cop with a hard-nose look immediately flashing his cruiser light in my face. The young cop waived him off indicating he had everything under control as he walked back to his car to run my information but the old vet kept his eye on me the entire time. My heart was pounding like African drums in my chest. I just knew this old geaser was going to snatch me out of my car and find my goodies.

After a few minutes the young cop came back with my info. "Ok Mr. Pazzaro you're clean. Just be sure to get that headlamp fixed and stop cheating on your fiancé."

"I sure will and thanks again. Is it ok if I make a u-turn here and head back to Philly?" "Yeah, go ahead. I'll block you."

He put on his overhead lights blocking the street as I made a u-turn and headed back to Philly. That little traffic stop could have landed me 5-7 years in the joint. (thank you angle)

The following week I went back to Marnissa's house while Yalanna was at my house. I told her I'd be home after the club around

3am. After our love making session I accidentally fell asleep and woke up around 7am. I jumped up and put on my clothes running out to my car and peeled off. I didn't know what I was going to tell Yalanna since I didn't have an alibi. On the way home I tried to contact Jones and Zack to have them help me make up a lie but neither of them were responding to my pages. I thought real hard and came up with a plan. My last resort was the hospital. I went straight to the emergency room.

"What can we do for you today Sir?," the nurse asked while putting a pressure cuff around my arm. She was a fat older white lady who looked like she'd been a nurse forever.

With my best I'm in pain impression, " My stomach is killing me nurse. I think I might have been food poisoned," bending over as if the pain was excruciating.

The nurse took my vital sighs and put a hospital band with my name on it around my wrist.

"Your pressure is normal and you don't have a fever," she said as she removed the cuff. Try to relax in the waiting room for a little while until we get an empty room and some one will be with you shortly."

As I walked away slowly bent over towards the waiting area, I looked behind me to make sure the nurse wasn't looking and I headed straight towards the exit door. The hospital band was all I needed.

When I got to my apartment around 8:45 am Yalanna was waiting in the living room furious.

"Where in the hell were you all night! I paged you at least 15 times!"

All I did was stick out my wrist exposing my hospital band.

"I know baby, I was in the hospital all night with a high fever," bending over holding my stomach.

If These Streets Could Talk

When she looked at my wrist and seen my hospital band she instantly became sympathetic.

"Aw I'm sorry G! I thought you was out with one of those chicken heads with Zack and Jones."

"Well I was with them at first but when we were out I started to feel lightheaded and Jones dropped me off at the hospital, didn't he call you and tell you?"

"I don't know. I was trying to call you all night. Maybe he was trying to reach me and couldn't get through."

She helped me into the bathroom and made me a hot bath. Afterwards she made me some homemade chicken soup and helped me into the bed.

"Now you get some rest and I'll be back later to check on you."

As I laid in bed I started thinking about how tired I was always lying to Yalanna about my whereabouts. Being a player was a full time job. That's when I decided I needed to stop the games. The next day I finally told Yalanna.

"I got a lot on my mind right now and I think that it would be best for us to part for a while until I figure this thing out. It's not you, it's me" When someone gives you that sorry line it means it's over.

It was a very sorry line but just like that after all that we've been through, I dumped Yalanna for Marnissa. Yalanna was devastated but my insensitivity didn't allow me to care. All I wanted was to be with Marnissa full time.

The following Saturday night when I rolled up at Heavy Hitters with Marnissa my boys couldn't believe their eyes. You see taking your main girl to the club is acceptable because every once in a while we all had to do it just to keep the peace. But to bring a girl other than your main girl to the club broke all the rules in the player handbook. Players **never** bring sand to the beach.

Zack saw me and pulled me to the side.

"G did you lose your damn mind? What in the hell are you doing bringing a freak to the freak nik?"

"Look Zack, this is my new woman so accept it and respect it. Me and Yalanna are history so give Nis the same props that you would give Yalanna."

Zack gave me the I'm stupid look.

"Man that girl must suck it off and put it back on or she put some roots on your dumb ass because you're showing signs of schizophrenia but hey, if that's the way you want it, then that's on you. If you choose to kick it with a chicken head then pluck on."

He walked away.

I stood there a little disturbed by his comment but didn't consider the fact that he might be right. I was convinced that Marnissa a winner.

After two months of unprotected sex with Marnissa, she finally said those dreadful words.

" G, I'm pregnant."

I didn't sweat it because she always said if it were to happen that she would get an abortion. Plus it was her idea of me not wearing a condom anyway always complaining that she was allergic to latex.

I told Marnissa to set up the day that she wants me to take her to the termination clinic so she made an appointment for the following week.

The abortion clinic has got to be one of the most disturbing places I have ever been in. When we first entered the parking lot the anti-abortion protesters attacked us calling us baby killers and murderers. They were pushing us and trying to convince Marnissa not to go through with it. It wasn't until I lifted my shirt up in the front exposing my gun that they backed off of us.

Inside the clinic I sat in my chair observing all of the young woman and girls in the room. Some appeared to be 13 and 14 years old looking like babies themselves and others just looked totally relaxed like getting an abortion was their means of birth control. As I looked around the waiting room there was this uncomfortable silence that was driving me crazy.

"Marnissa Simmons, the nurse called and escorted her into the back. I thought to myself; "I didn't even know her last name was Simmons."

I recall dosing off in my chair and being awakened by a crying Marnissa. I stood up, wrapped my arms around her and held her tight. I assumed having an abortion could be pretty traumatic to a person so I tried to console her.

"It's alright Nis, lets go home," I said escorting her to the door.

Whipping her eyes, "G I didn't do it, I couldn't do it."

"What do you mean you couldn't do it," my whole attitude changed and so did hers.

" You got to do it," I yelled in her face.

"Oh I'm good enough to screw but I'm not good enough to have a baby by?"

That comment caught everyone in the waiting room's attention as all eyes were on us.

" Look, you better get you're ass back in that room and get on that table and let that doctor do what he got to do. I told you before I'm not having no kids!"

"Well you ain't got to worry about it, I'll take care of it myself."

The nurse ran over to us because we were yelling at the top of our lungs obviously upsetting the other people in the clinic. One young girl even ran out of the door crying as her mother ran behind her hollering for her to come back. The nurse stepped in between us.

"Why don't you two go home and talk it over and make sure that you're making the right decision. You can always reschedule another appointment," she said while escorting us towards the exit.

The car ride home was total chaos. We yelled and screamed at each other all of the way home. I couldn't believe that Marnissa didn't go through with the abortion. I only knew this girl for two and a half months and she insisted on having my baby. I was a twenty four year old drug dealer/womanizer. I was too selfish and self-centered to have a child. All I liked to do was drink, party, make money, drive my cars, stay well groomed, and sex women. The only thing important to me in life was me. Having a baby would ruin everything that I lived for.

When I got home I asked KK what I should do. She was the wrong person to ask since she totally opposed abortions.

"The bed you make in life is the one that you have to sleep in. Live with it," were her exact words.

Maria had four kids because KK refused to give her abortion money or have anything to do with the killing of a fetus. I'm surprised the kids even survived Marie's drug habit but I had four lovely nieces and nephews.

Banita thought the whole thing was funny. She always had a sick sense of humor.

"Well mister player man you thought you were so cool in your silk suits and flashy jewelry. Well guess what? You got played by a smutt, Ha Ha Ha Ha Ha Ha Ha." Then rubbing it in even more, "You know what? You are so stupid. You dropped Yalanna, the best thing that ever happened to your dog ass, just to hook up with a project bumb. I don't know what Yalanna ever even seen in you myself because you ain't nothing but a fake ass wanna be pimp. How could you hook up with a girl from Coatesville that you hardly even know and get her pregnant? You are a straight up NUT! Ha Ha Ha Ha ….."

I looked at her with disgust. I wanted so bad to choke her but she was right. Some how, some way, I had to get Marnissa to get this abortion. Even though Yalanna and I weren't together I still loved her and me having a baby by someone else would really break her heart. I dug deep down in my mental bank and came up with a plan.

I told Jones to come over my house so I could tell him my plan. "Now let me get this straight G." "You're going to give me $2,000 to push Nis down the El steps?"

"That's right. I'll send her to the mall and have her return on the three O'clock train. You wait for her at the top of the platform to get off of the El and when she does, I want you to walk behind her and shove her down those steps like you hate her. I don't care if you break her damn neck, just do it. I want her to have an instant abortion.

Jones smiled, "Man have my two grand in unmarked unsequential bills in a manila envelope. This is going to be the easiest cash that I ever made."

When Jones walked away I noticed that his pants were sagging in the butt. He was obviously loosing a lot of weight.

"You need to take some of that money and go food shopping. It looks like you're loosing you're ass." He turned around, "That's all right because after I make this money, it's going to be serf and turf on you my brotha."

I picked Nis up that Friday night and let her spend the night at my apartment. I didn't want to cause any suspicion so I took her to dinner and told her that everything was cool and I was ok with her having the baby.

After dinner we went my place and made love as usual. The next morning I told her to go to the mall to buy herself a winter coat since the weather was really dropping. Her being a shopaholic jumped up and immediately got dressed. I gave her $500 to go to the gallery to buy a coat.

"Make sure that you're back by three thirty because I have to make a run," I told her so my little plan could go accordingly.

"Ok Sweetie." She gave me a kiss and walked out of the door.

When she left out I immediately beeped Jones. He called me right back.

" Alright, the pigeon has left the cage and she'll be getting off of the El at three O'clock so be on post."

"Look here G.I. Joe, This ain't the Marines so kill all that pigeon and post shit. I got this thing under control. Just have my money ready before you go to the hospital.

"Hospital? Hospital for what?"

"Oh I'm pushing this bitch from the top steps. The hospital is going to be a must." We both just laughed and hung up the phone.

The anticipation was killing me. I felt like a kid the night before Christmas waiting for three thirty to come. At 3:05 I beeped Jones and he called me right back. "Anything happen yet?" I asked anxiously.

"Man where in the hell is this girl. It's cold as a witch's tit out here."

Trying to assure him, "be patient dude, she should definitely be on the next train. Just walk to my house when the job is done."

Fifteen minutes later my doorbell rang. I thought "man that was fast." I had Jones money in my pocket.

When I looked through the peephole I couldn't believe my eyes. It was Nis with shopping bags in her hands.

"Hurry up and open the door I got to pee," she said dancing around in circles. I hesitated in disbelief then opened the door. She ran past me dropping her bags on the floor and headed straight into the bathroom. "I'm glad you gave me money to buy a coat," she said panting out of breath. "It's freezing out there." "What took you so long to come back," trying not to show how annoyed I was to see her. "Oh I caught a cab. I didn't feel like walking up all of those El steps." The phone rang; it was Jones. "Yo. "It's three thirty five and three trains went by and my nuts are frozen solid." I cut him off. "Forget it man, she's here."

"What do you mean she's there? There ain't no way she got by me." Whispering into the phone. "I know man she caught a cab." "So what does that mean I don't get paid?" "Yeah, that's right, I'm not paying you for an unaccomplished mission." "Now wait a minute. It's not my fault that she diverted her schedule and caught a cab." "Well it's not my fault either," obviously sounding just as annoyed as he was. "Look man, I'm freezing my balls off out here trying to save you a life time of hell so you can at least give me half." "Are you crazy? I'm not giving you shit," I said in a louder whisper. "Well then put her on the phone so I can tell her that you just tried to have her and her baby executed."

I thought for a second,

"Alright man I'll give you half but you better not tell nobody about our murder attempt."

"Mums the word baby boy. Just give me my dough," he said with what I could tell a smile on his face.

I hung up the phone.

In my bedroom Marnissa was so excited showing me some of the maternity clothes that she had bought. I acted like I was interested and excited but inside I was pissed. "Damn," I thought. "She must have an angel too."

If These Streets Could Talk

Ch 15   Thou Shall Not Covet Thy Neighbor's House

It was about 11:30 pm and we usually closed down our business at midnight. Maria's kids were still up running around the apartment playing and she was somewhere on the streets but nowhere to be found. KK was winding down working on her fourth glass of Bacardi light since it was near closing time. Clear was counting KK's money, making sure that him and her were coming up with the same amount. Me and Banita were sitting on the couch watching" Good Times" when the doorbell rang.

Clear went to the door thinking it was just another customer.

"KK after this one I'm locking the door, I'm tired. " "Well so am I," KK said while sipping her rum.

Clear was also drinking some rum as he opened the front door. Through the security gate he saw it was Maria and her girlfriend Sharon who was also a known crack addict. " Oh shit, it's just the walking dead," Clear announced turning his back to them after opening the gate.

When they walked in I had an instant bad feeling. My first impression was that they were high from the blank looks that they had on their faces. Then behind them were three guys that I had never seen before. When Clear seen them he turned around and stuck his hand out.

"Yo ya'll can't come in right now, no company."

The fat dark-skinned one with the beard and dirty white baseball cap pulled out a .38 caliber.

"We ain't company. This here is a stick up," putting his other hand right at the front of Clear's pants knowing exactly where he kept his gun disarming him.

Banita screamed, "Shut your damn mouth!" The skinny one said pointing the gun at Banita.

147

I knew instantly this wasn't good. My mind immediately went to work. You see, I had pulled off and seen plenty of stick-ups. Some where people got shot and some even killed. I knew I had to do something to take control of this situation to assure my family's safety without getting anyone killed.

"Alright everybody lie down on the floor," the short one demanded pushing Maria and her girlfriend to the floor. Maria's kids were looking confused so I grabbed the two youngest ones.

"Lie down on the floor with Uncle G," I said trying to pretend that I was playing a game with them. Although her other two sons were eight and ten years old, they were streetwise and knew exactly what was going on so they obeyed every order.

As the skinny one went into the back where KK was, I could tell Clear started to tackle him but with my eyes and facial language I pleaded with him not to do anything so he laid on the floor still sipping his drink.

"What do ya'll want man? We only make twos and fews in here. There ain't no real money in here," I said trying to sound convincing.

He pulled me up to my feet by my shirt while pointing the gun at my head. "Well then show me were you keep the twos and fews little nigga."

As he was escorting me to the back of the apartment where KK was, our cat Charles, ran out of the bedroom really startling him because he jumped almost dropping his gun. Right then and there I knew that he was an amateur. Real stick up men would have killed any unknown thing that moved. I knew then that I had a chance of walking through this thing without anyone getting hurt. These were just chumps with guns.

His friends had the rest of my family at gunpoint in the living room.

"Ya"ll making a big mistake, Ya"ll robbing' the wrong people," Clear warned them.

The little one hit Clear in the head with the butt of his gun.

"Shut your damn mouth fool!"

Clear took the blow to the head without even flinching then took another sip of his rum while lying on his stomach.

In the back, KK was emptying out the closet were we kept our stash while fat boy had the gun pointed at her. Fat boy grabbed KK's shirtsleeve.

"This better be everything or I'll kill everybody in here!"

Blood quickly filled my head watching him point a gun and then grabbing the sleeve of the person who I loved more than life itself.

Disregarding the fact that he was armed I turned to him and looked him dead in his eye.

"Don't grab my moms like that again. Just take the weed and get out of here." He looked in my eyes obviously intimidated but pulled a trash bag out of his jacket pocket and put the two pounds of weed and about $8,600 in cash that KK had surrendered to him. I thought to myself, This nigga had a trash bag in his damn pocket; he must have been looking forward to this being a good payday".

The two-rookie stick up men took KK and me back into the living room where everyone else was still lying on the floor. Fat boy put his gun up to my temple.

"I'm telling ya'll that if I find out that yawl are holding back on me I'm going to blow his fucking head off!"

" Look man, ya"ll got the money so just get the hell out. I'm starting to get mad!" Clear blurted out as if he couldn't restrain his anger anymore.

"Didn't I tell you to shut your damn mouth?" the short one said hitting Clear in the head again with the butt of his gun again. Clear just grunted, burped, and took another sip of his rum.

Then for some unknown reason Banita took it upon herself to say, "We have some more up stairs, just don't hurt anybody."

Now I knew that she was afraid because I was too but I couldn't believe she actually directed them upstairs to my apartment foiling my whole plan. I had already figured after they left the building, I would run upstairs to the third floor and shoot them from out of my window. Fat boy smiled.

"Well let's go then."

Fat boy and skinny man walked behind me and Banita as we all walked up the stairs. The third chump kept my family at bay on the second floor.

Upstairs in my apartment they took everything that they could carry using my laundry bag to transport the goods. They took my video camera, my diamond infested Rolex watch that I had sitting on my coffee table and several other things I had lying around. They even found the rifle and my 9mm that I had planned on killing them with.

Once again Banita's scary ass directed them to the $30,000 I had in a shoebox in the back of my closet. Thank God she didn't know about my floor safe or I wouldn't have had nothing left.

Fat boy had a nerve to ask me, "You don't mind if I take this Scarface tape do you," while going through my movie collection.

" No problem as long as you return it, it's my favorite," I responded sarcastically.

After they finished tearing my place up they took us back to the second floor with their bags full of my goodies.

"Alright, everybody stay calm. We're going to take him with us for a little ride (referring to me) and if everybody stays cool, he'll be back shortly."

It looked like everybody in the room burst into tears. The kids were pulling at my pants leg begging the bandits not to take me. Clear who was the only one not crying was yelling at the bandits.

"Let him stay and take me! Take me man! Take me!"

"All right everybody shut the hell up before I blast him!" Fat boy pointed the gun at my head. I tried to calm everybody down.

"Stop crying, "I'm going to be alright," I said while tearing my nieces and nephews off of my legs.

"It's ok, Uncle G will be right back."

They closed the door and had their guns pointed at me as I led the way down stairs.

In the back of my mind I was looking forward to getting outside because I knew that when my boys saw me walking out of my building with three unfamiliar faces to the neighborhood, it would definitely cause suspicion and then action would be taken.

Well to my surprise outside of my building was like a ghost town. It had just finished pouring rain. No one was outside, not even the regular crack heads. The streets were dark, quiet, and deserted like these jerks knew exactly when to hit our house.

"Alright, we're going to take a little walk around the corner," fat boy said shoving me in the back with the nose of his gun for me to move.

At that point my legs just stopped. Fat boy pushed his hard steel into my lower back indicating that I'd better keep walking but I thought about what could happen if I get into their car and I wasn't going. You see in the car they have the upper hand. In the car my fate lies in their hands. They could beat me or shoot me or do anything they wanted to me in the car. Case always said never allow yourself to get kidnapped because when you're abducted, chances are greater that your abductors kill you. Believe me I was afraid but I was not getting into that car.

Pushing his gun harder into my back, the little one said. "You better keep you're ass moving."

I stopped walking.

"I'm not getting in no car!"

"I said move it!"

He pushed me again. I refused to move. I figured at least if they kill me on my porch I could have a decent burial. If I get in the car they might find my body weeks later out in the woods all decomposed and I'll have to have a closed casket funeral.

Fat boy finally gave up and walked away slowly still pointing the gun at me.

"Stay right there and don't move," still pointing the gun at me from a distance.

When they reached the bottom of the stairs they took off running like the cowards I knew they were. I ran back up to the second floor and when I opened the door everybody jumped on me hugging and kissing me. KK was crying which was rare.

"I thought I wasn't ever going to see you again," she said hugging me.

Clear was already on the phone with Maynard and his hit squad informing them about the robbery and attempted abduction giving them a full description of the culprits.

In less than thirty minuets about twenty-five gun-toting warriors were on the "W" ready for action. Maynard questioned Maria and Sharon suspecting them of a possible set up.

"If I find out that yawl had anything to do with this I'm going to torture ya'll both Japanese style," he assured them. Of course they denied having anything to do with it knowing that the consequences of betrayal is death and Maynard was crazy enough to do it.

Since we all were together I decide to go to the speakeasy (a place where they sell illegal alcohol) and buy a few cases of beer and wine. All of us sat outside all night long and drank and talked the night away.

If These Streets Could Talk

Ch 16 We Know Not What We Do

After the robbery, we became extra cautious about who we let in and out of our building. We even hired my boy Sarge who was a sharp shooter in the Army to sit outside and watch out for any suspicious activities. Once it's known on the streets that your place has been hit it makes you vulnerable for a possible second attack. Even though the three amigos that hit us were fake-ass thugs they stung us hard for an estimated $80,000 in weed and cash not including miscellaneous items like my jewelry and guns.

I had an APB on the streets wanting any information leading to the whereabouts of the robbers. I knew deep down inside that it was probably an inside job by no other than Maria but I didn't press the issue since I knew what Maynard would have done to her. Even though she had an addiction problem she was still my sister and I loved her.

After the robbery I stayed closer to home. Nis was about five months pregnant at this time and we were in my bedroom play fighting which was something that she always liked to do. When I flipped her in the air I accidentally fell on top of her landing all of my weight on her stomach. She screamed while running into the bathroom holding her stomach in obvious pain.

"G I'm bleeding," she said through the door while crying. I knew that wasn't a good sign so I called down stairs to KK.

"You know that if that girl is bleeding that she most likely lost that baby. You need to take her to the hospital right away." What's wrong with you wrestling with that girl knowing that she's pregnant?"

"Well, it's too late now," I said. "Let me call you right back."

When I hung up the phone I was full of joy. If I would have known that flipping her would make her loose that baby, I would have suplexed her a long time ago.

I escorted her to the car and took her to the emergency room. She was crying the whole time. "You did that on purpose," she said while sitting in the car holding her stomach.

Trying to act sympathetic. "Why would I do something like that to you? Look, you were the one who wanted to play WWF." Knowing deep down inside I didn't have any regrets or remorse for the termination of this unwanted child.

Marnissa and I were sitting inside of a room in the ER waiting for her test results from the ultrasound. After a series of tests the doctor came out with the results. "Miss Simmons, you should really consider yourself extremely lucky. Our tests indicate that you could have caused considerable damage to the fetus from the pressure of the fall that you encountered but miraculously you didn't receive any internal damage. I highly suggest that in the future you avoid any other type of horseplay or any other strenuous or physical activities."

I was pissed! Here I am thinking that I gave her an instant abortion and super baby just took a blow to the head and shook it off like it was nothing. When things are meant to be they are just meant to be. I came to the conclusion that I was going to be a father but wasn't happy about it. Further more, how was I going to tell Yalanna.

"She's pregnant?"

Yalanna yelled into the phone at the top of her lungs.

"How could you get that girl pregnant after all we've been through? Why wasn't your nasty ass wearing a condom?"

"I was but it busted." Knowing that I was lying.

"I'm telling you right now, if she has that baby you can forget about ever even knowing me."

She hung up the phone with a bang. I knew Yalanna was really hurt because about a year ago I convinced her to have an abortion.

Afterwards she was really depressed knowing she killed an unborn child.

After I thought about it, I remember Octavia, Barbara, Rose and Sandra having aborted my seed also. I loved Yalanna and didn't want to lose her. Marnissa and me were cool but she was no Yalanna. Although Yalanna and I were young we had some great times traveling different places and growing together. I wanted her back and I knew how I would get her. A trip to Jamaica.

I told Yalanna about the trip. At first she was a little hesitant but I knew traveling was one of her weaknesses. She always loved to go different places, eat different foods, and learn different cultures. I told her to make all of the traveling arrangements and I'll handle all of the expenses.

Of course KK opposed of the idea of me being gone for a week knowing I was the only person she could trust one hundred percent but after I explained to her that I was trying to win Yalanna back she understood.

I also made sure everything was in order when I left bagging enough weed to sell for ten days. I gave Clear authority over things until I returned.

"Man you know I'm going to hold things down until you come back G. Just be sure to bring me back some of that Jamaican rum. They tell me that stuff puts hair on your chest."

Even though Clear wasn't the sharpest knife in the drawer, I knew I could trust him because he was loyal. He'd proved on several occasions that he's willing to put his life on the line for our family. Plus I told Jones to keep an eye out on things and gave him an ounce of weed to assure the job would be done.

We had to catch our flight out of Kennedy airport in NY so I had a limousine pick us up on the "W" and take us to the airport.

If These Streets Could Talk

You should have seen Yalanna and me looking like stars leaving the neighborhood limo style. I told Marnissa that I was going down south for a week because my aunt had died and left me some property that I had to take care of. She was hurt that I was leaving for so many days but I was sure that the $1,000 I gave her helped to ease the pain.

That was the worst flight that I have ever flown. They served us stale peanuts and warm soda. We also experienced turbulence and hit so many air pockets that I thought we were going to die for sure.

Since our hotel was in Ocho Rios, which was the furthest island from the airport, we had to ride in this dirty old school bus through a dirty old town to the resort area. Riding through the town was really upsetting seeing the malnutrition animals and grass huts. I told Yalanna I thought we should go back but she insisted on continuing.

The ride was so bumpy that my video camera fell from the overhead compartment on the bus and hit a little girl on the head, which didn't require any stitches but left her with a large lump on her head. I felt horrible and couldn't apologize enough to her and her family. I even gave them $100 for the trouble.

Once we hit the hotel in Ocho Rios it was a totally different atmosphere. The hotel was beautiful and immaculate. Inside waterfalls, marble floors, and our room had the most breath taking ocean side view. At first I didn't like the fact that our room didn't have a T.V but our hostess assured us that there were so many activities that there wasn't any time for television.

On the beach I was amazed at how I could actually see my feet right through the crystal clear water. Too bad I didn't see the jellyfish that stung me on my stomach, which turned out to be ok since it gave me a chance to flirt with the island nurse.

I also made the mistake of drinking the water in Jamaica, which sent me back to the island nurse with a fever and diarrhea. She gave me the smallest little white pill and in an hour I was back to partying on the beach.

Everywhere we went in Jamaica somebody would try to sell us weed not knowing that I too was in the same business.

This one dude who called himself Dr. Biology approached me with a hard Jamaican accent.

"Come help a brotha out and buy sum ganja Mon."

I figured I'd throw it right back at him.

"Me don't smoke ganja mon. Back in the states me sell ganja too."

"Well then brudgren, you know me need the money plus it's written all over your face that you do smoke. I can see it in your eyes."

Now I don't know what he thought he saw in my eyes since I hadn't smoked ganja for years but I just laughed and gave him $20 just for being so smooth.

Just then it started to rain and as I ran for cover Dr. Biology yells to me, "what you runnin for Mon. It never rains in Jamaica. It's just liquid sunshine."

Liquid sunshine sounded so cool to me that I stopped running and just absorbed nature's gift from the sky.

In Jamaica me and Yalanna fell deeper in love. We parasailed, jet skied, snorkeled, and went glass boat fishing. We climbed Dun River Falls and the food was unexplainably fresh and delicious and the drinks were made to perfection.

We let the waves splash against our feet as we walked on the pure white sand holding hands on the beach at night. "Giovanni I don't want to loose you but it's hard for me to except the fact that you're having a baby by someone other than me. I did a lot of thinking and I decided to stick by your side if you promise to leave that Marnissa girl alone and just take care of your child."

" Baby if that's all that I have to do then consider it done."

Between how good Yalanna looked in her bikini and the Jamaican air and atmosphere, you couldn't tell me that when we made love I wasn't seeing fire works. Who ever said "Come back to Jamaica and make it your home" didn't have to tell me twice. I will be back.

If These Streets Could Talk

Ch. 17 Going Nowhere Fast

One week later we arrived back in Philly at about 4:00pm. Yalanna's skin had a cocoa brown glow to it from the island sun. I, on the other hand, looked like the ace of spades with my extra dark skin and course hair. The cab driver dropped Yalanna off first then took me to the "W".

At my building I crept up the stairs past KK's apartment so I could at least unpack before she put me back to work.

I hadn't even stepped through the door when the phone rang. Sounding obviously annoyed I answered it.

"Hello."

It was Banita sounding frantic.

"Why didn't you tell me that you were home? I thought you weren't coming home until tonight."

"That's why I told you tonight so you wouldn't bother me. Why you sound out of breath, what's up?"

"What's up is Maria has been missing for five days, KK's in jail, and Case is dead."

I sat down on the arm of my couch since I felt weakness in my knees that almost enabled me to stand. I wanted to ask her to repeat what she had said but I didn't really want to hear it again.

"I'll be right down," I hanging up the phone.

Downstairs Banita told me everything with her eyes full of tears.

"Alright, now we all know Case was smoking crack but we didn't know he turned into a first class crack head. Well word got back to Maynard that he was the one who set us up when we got robbed."

"How do you know?"

160

"Because the guys that robbed us were some of Case's smoker buddies from down the bottom and one of them leaked out the information to one of Maynard's workers. You know the streets talk."

I thought about how Case always said, "If it doesn't come out in the wash, it comes out in the rinse," and it did. Didn't he know that the streets don't lie. Maynard was too deep in the streets not to find out who robbed us.

She continued. "Now you know how Maynard feels about being double-crossed. Well word on the street is he took Case out to Fairmont Park, tied him to a tree, and shot him nine times."

She started crying even harder

"Case didn't deserve to die like that G. Plus they said Maynard caught the other three guys and tied them up in an abandoned building and set it on fire. G I don't like Maynard and I'm afraid of him. He's sick. He didn't have to do that to Case. He was our big brother man."

The tears rolled down the side of her face profusely as she spoke. I wanted to cry also but my body wouldn't allow a tear to come out. Yalanna always thought I had a mental problem because I never cried, not even at funerals. Case, on the other hand, was the only man in my life that ever showed me love. He wasn't **like** a big brother to me, he **was** my brother. He taught me the only thing that he knew which was how to survive in the streets. I wish he had taken his own advice. He knew if he needed anything he could have came to me or KK. Even if he was the one who set us up I still loved him. When people are hooked on crack they'll do anything to anybody to get it. It's an uncontrollable addiction that totally takes over your mind and body. The loyalest family member will double-cross his or her own mother.

She continued,----

"Then on Saturday night around 8:00 Clear asked me to watch the door while he ran to the bar to get a beer. When the doorbell rang I just thought it was just Clear returning. When I opened it, this big white dude had a shotgun pointed at me telling me to lie on the ground. I thought it was another stickup. I heard a loud crash like somebody breaking down the back door. Man they had the dickey boys all through our apartment taking any and every thing. Since you weren't here KK never made a trip to the bank to make a deposit so she had about $175,000 cash although they said it was only $45,000. And they found about six pounds of weed. I told them that it was mine and that I would take the rap, but then this dude that I remember seeing buying from us plenty of times before, but now I realize that he was a undercover, said that he had bought some weed from KK personally so they took her away."

I tried to compose myself to take in all of her information.

" So where's Clear now?"

"When he was coming from the bar he seen 5-0 surrounding our building and made a U turn. I haven't seen him since."

"What about Jones?"

" He stopped by once while you were gone but I haven't seen him for a few days. Last time I seen him he was looking kind of sick."

"Why didn't you bail KK out?"

"I tried to but when I went to the bank they said she didn't have any available funds. I don't know where Maria is. She left her kids at her piper girlfriend's house and disappeared. What are we going to do G?" She burst into tears.

I wiped the tears from her eyes and embraced her. Neither Case nor KK would want me folding under pressure. It took a lot out of me but I immediately blocked out the fact that Case was dead. He always told me to never worry about things that are out of your control.

The first thing that I had to do was get KK out of jail. The thought of Maria withdrawing all of KK's money out of the bank made me sick to my stomach but the thought of KK being in jail made me even sicker.

I called Maynard's girlfriend's house since I knew he'd be there. Even though he was married with three kids he had a totally separate life with this young girl out in Germantown. I needed to hear it from him personally that he killed Case.

Unsympathetically." That's right G; I had to take him out. He betrayed the family and it couldn't be overlooked."

I was furious.

"Man who the hell made you judge and jury. You're not God! You can't go around deciding who lives and who dies. You killed my brother motherfucker!"

Maynard sounded upset. "You better slow your roll G," he said with that deep killer voice. "I did what I had to do. If I had let him get away with robbing my family anybody would try us. Now take it on the chin and deal with it because if I even think you plan on ratting me out, you can get some heat too, dig me? Now can I trust you or not?"

At first I hesitated. I had nothing but hate and resentment for Maynard but since I didn't want to be placed on his "people to kill" list I thought it best to go along with it. "Yeah you can trust me, "I said and I hung up the phone.

KK's bail was set at $100,000, which meant that I had to pay $10,000. I didn't care if I had to use it all I just needed to see her.

When they released her she didn't look well. Her hair was a mess and her sweat suit was dirty. She had bags under her eyes and even though it was just two days she even looked like she dropped a few pounds. I ran up to her and hugged her for what felt like an eternity. I could tell she wanted to cry but refused to in public.

In my car KK broke down. I pulled my car over to console her.

"I don't want to do this anymore," KK said wiping the tears away from under her glasses. "Maria stole all of the money out of my account and Case lost his life. This is blood money; it's wicked and evil and I don't want any parts of it."

"Alright Mom I agree too, but we have to take care of a few things. First we get a good lawyer to handle your case. The last thing you need is time in the pen. Then we give Case a decent burial and I find out where Maria is hiding out at." She agreed so we drove home and I cooked her favorite dinner. Steak, potatoes, and a salad.

If These Streets Could Talk

Ch 18 Amazing Grace

"Where in the hell have you been all week? I'm at the hospital with Marnissa and she's about to have your baby and you just disappear. My sister didn't get pregnant by herself so get your ass down here now!"

Marnissa's sister was in total violation calling me like this not knowing with everything going on I was like a bomb with a short fuse. She hardly even knew me well enough to be calling my house with the ghetto tough girl approach. Obviously she didn't know that all I had to do was make one phone call to get her jaw broken and her big mouth wired up for a month. I didn't have any love for Marnissa but as much as I hated it the fact still remained that she was having my baby.

"Look, just call me when the baby is born. I'm having a lot of problems over here right now and I don't need your added stress so you better get off of me,"

She obviously didn't care.

"We don't need your crap either so.." I just hung up the phone.

That afternoon I got a visit from my crack head informant Smitty. I let him in and as usual he was dirty, smelly, itching and couldn't stand still. It's sad because Smitty used to be a mailman but got hooked up with the wrong people during his lunch breaks. They convinced him that crack would keep him going while he delivered the mail.

In a matter of nine months Smitty lost his BMW jeep, single home, wife, kids, teeth, manhood, and spirit. Now he does odd jobs around the neighborhood for a few dollars. I mean he'll do anything. I seen Smitty clean out a pit bull cage full of mountains of shit. Thing is, he did it with his bare hands all for $20!

"Yo G. I saw Maria last night at the Ithan St. crackhouse. She was spending a lot of money on dope talking about she hit the number."

"Are you sure?"

"Man I get high but I ain't blind. Me and your sister got high plenty of times. Yes I'm sure. Now can I get a few dollars for my information?"

I gave him $20 and he snatched it from my hand and ran down the stairs.

I got dressed and headed to Maria's location.

I knocked on the door looking around at how disgusting the front porch was. It had a dirty old couch on it with beer cans and wine bottles scattered everywhere. It also had used condoms on it letting me know it wasn't used for just sitting. Some of the window were broken out replaced with trash bags and duct tape.

When the malnutrition dread-lock wearing lady opened the door, I almost vomited from the cocaine fumes.

"Where's Maria," I asked putting my hand over my nose and mouth to block out some of the fumes. Looking at me like she didn't know who I was talking about she said,

"I haven't seen her but what can I do for you," she asked licking her tongue in a circular motion. I restrained myself from vomiting.

"You can't do shit for me at all! Look, just tell her," I paused as I looked behind her through the crack of the door .The house was dark and smokey but I was still able to see Maria sitting on another raggedy couch begging some guy sitting next to her to hurry up and give her the pipe. I pushed mop head to the side and the door swung opened. Maria was so out of her mind that she didn't even notice me coming her way. Smack! I slapped her in the back of her head.

Dropping her peace pipe she turned around holding her head to see who hit her. Smack! I slapped her again this time in her face.

"What the hell is wrong with you stealing KK's money and abandoning your kids just to get high!"

As she looked up and saw me realizing I was the one who hit her, her eyes lit up like two light bulbs.

As she got up off of the floor and tried to make a run for the door. I tripped her and she fell again. Meanwhile a couple of people ran out of the house while some others continued to smoke like nothing was happening. The guy that was sitting on the couch next to her stood up like he was going to do something. He was tall but looked thin and unhealthy assuring me that if I had too, I could take him with one hard punch.

You're going to have to take that stupid shit outside young boy. You're blowing my high with all of that hype Clint Eastwood shit!"

I pulled my gun out and pointed it at him.

"Look man, this is a family matter. You're not family, so you don't matter."

He dropped his pipe and ran out the front door.

I grabbed Maria by the hair and led her to the door. On a norm I would have never treated my sister this way but under the circumstances she was overdue for an ass whippin'.

When we got outside in the light I looked down at her stomach and couldn't believe that she was pregnant again especially after she had her last son in KK's living room. She was so high on crack that day that she didn't even feel any contractions when my nephew came out on the living room floor.

Looking wild and uncivilized, "Whatcha gonna do kill me? Don't you think I'm tired of living like this too?"

She started crying.

"How do you think I feel with four kids and their father ain't nowhere to be found? I dropped out of school in the seventh grade and don't have nothing. You and KK so busy selling that damned weed ya'll don't even see that I have problems. If you're going to kill me then go ahead and do it because I don't want to live like this no more anyway."

She fell to her knees on the sidewalk. I pulled her up and embraced her. Even though she was a crack head she was still my little sister and nothing would ever change that. Case always told me that you have to be patient when it comes to family because they put you through tests that no one else would. I put her in my car and took her home.

The next morning my phone rang around 2:30 am. It was Marnissa's sister again.

"What in the hell is your problem calling my house this time of night?" I yelled through the phone.

"Marnissa just had a girl," she said. "Your sorry ass is a father."

Still half asleep. "Yeah, yeah whatever. I'll be there in the morning."

"No, see that's where you're wrong. What you need to do is come over here right now and …" I hung up.

The next day I will never forget for the rest of my life. July 15, 1991. The same day as my grandmother's birthday. Banita and me rode out to Coatesville Medical to see my so-called daughter.

" Man are you sure that this baby is yours?" Banita asked during our car ride to the hospital. "That girl Marnissa seems a little scandalous. She doesn't look like no one man woman to me."

In agreement with her. "I can't believe it either but yeah I'm pretty sure but I still have to see it to believe it."

If These Streets Could Talk

At the hospital I was a nervous wreck. Banita walked in Marnissa's room first with her phony smile.

"Congratulations girl! Can I hold her," reaching for the baby knowing she only wanted to determine any family resemblance.

Marnissa was holding the baby on her chest lying in the bed. She raised the bed up and slowly handed the baby to Banita obviously in pain.

Babies sure take a toll on some women because Nis looked totally different. Her nose was about three times the regular size and her neck was five shades darker. Also, her hair and fingernails looked like they actually grew. And even though she had just given birth, her stomach was still poked as if she were still pregnant.

"I'm glad to see that you decided to come," Marnissa said to me sarcastically, " I don't know why you're trippen, she looks just like you."

Banita took the baby.

"Damn G, this is definitely your baby."

Still having a negative attitude I reached out for the new born baby.

"Let me see her."

She handed her to me.

"Make sure you hold her head," Marnissa said.

" Look, I got four nieces and nephews that I help raise. One thing that I do know is how to hold a baby."

I took the baby and gently removed her hat. When I looked down what I saw and felt was astonishing. I was actually holding a mini me. Her eyes and nose were a miniature version of mine. She even had my big forehead. It sent a chill through my entire body. I've never felt anything like it before.

"Her name is Ania in case you wanted to know."

If These Streets Could Talk

I totally ignored her, as I looked down at my mini me. She looked so content lying in my arms as if I were the protector of her entire world. I fell instantly in love with her. I was speechless. I couldn't do anything but hold and stare at her in amazement. All that was going through my mind was that this little girl is really a part of me and she will have nothing but the best. Isn't it funny how you spend your whole life putting yourself first, and then all of a sudden you're second.

If These Streets Could Talk

Ch 19 A Voice Of Reasoning

The day of Case's funeral was one of the saddest days of my life. He was too young to be dead. Case always said "You live fast, die young, and make a beautiful corpse, except he was the corpse.

The funeral was at a huge church Case's Aunt attended and it must have been over three hundred people in attendance. My heart was torn in pieces and the entire day I had a pounding headache and couldn't eat anything. I thought about how I really resented Maynard for killing Case and just walking around the streets like nothing ever happened.

Even though Maynard was my cousin I was hoping somebody would do to him what he had done to Case but I didn't know anybody brave or crazy enough to do it. Maynard was a known killer who everybody feared and respected.

Everyone around the neighborhood came to the funeral to pay their last respect to Case. He was definitely a neighborhood legend in spite of his recent drug addiction.

I sat in the very back of the church since I couldn't stand seeing Case lying in a casket. I observed as people came up one by one getting a final view of the man I always considered my hero. Surprisingly Clear even showed up to the funeral. I hadn't seen him since KK got locked up.

When he saw me, Clear came over to me, gave me a hug, and whispered in my ear.

"Sorry G man, one love baby." I looked in his eyes and he too looked like he too had been up crying all night.

I couldn't say anything but I'm sure the look on my face let him know that seeing him made me feel a little better.

If These Streets Could Talk

As people were viewing Case's body I noticed this one lady walking down the isle with what appeared to be an angry look on her face. Although she was well dressed there was something about her that didn't seem right. I kept my focus on her as she approached the casket.

She was about in her mid forties to early fifties. She was wearing all black, which made her thin build look even thinner, almost anorexic. And although she was wearing a hat, her tacky wig was exposed under it to show her lack of class. She was also walking a little uneasy in her stiletto heals.

When it was her turn to pay her respects to Case, she approached the casket, bent over and looked down at him. Then in a loud voice she said, " You no good bastard, go straight to hell!" Then slapped Case's face so hard that you could hear it echo throughout the entire church.

Now maybe he did something to her or to her daughter in the past or maybe he owed her some money or something. Whatever the reason was I don't know. All I do know is that all hell broke loose.

It looked like half of the people in the church jumped on this unknown lady and commenced to beat her down. The pastor was up on the podium yelling into the microphone trying to tell everyone to calm down while the ushers were getting punched in the cross fire trying to save the lady. Two of Case's cousins just dragged the unknown lady down the center of the isle with her shoes and wig off and dress torn to shreds all the way through the church and out the door.

There was so much commotion going on I couldn't believe that I was at a funeral. Me and everyone else were in disbelief at what had just taken place.

When I looked up at the podium the pastor had his eyes closed. I assumed he was praying for peace and order of this melee. Then out of nowhere he started to hum the most beautiful hum that I had ever heard come out of a human being totally capturing my attention then he started to sing.

"Praaaaay for meeeeee. Praaaaaaay, praaaay for meeeee. When you walk up to that alterrrrrrr please, please, please, don't forget to praaaaay for meeeeee hhmmmm hmmmm hmmmmm ."

His voice was soul touching. Angelic

Although everyone around me was yelling, fussing, cursing, and fighting, I could only hear his voice. The more he sang the more the crowd slowly settled down until eventually everybody was back in their seats as if they were hypnotized by his vocal healing. My body was riddled with goose bumps from the power of his voice and from the looks of things, I wasn't the only one. It was definitely a spiritually moving moment.

The pastor went on and continued the sermon talking about how Jesus died on the cross for our sins and how we have to be born again to enter the kingdom of heaven. He also prayed for Case in hope that somewhere in his sin filled life style he accepted Jesus Christ as his personal savior so he too could inherit the kingdom of heaven. For some reason my focus was no longer on Case but on the pastor and what he was saying. It was a funeral that I would never forget.

If These Streets Could Talk

Ch 20 I Surrender

KK's lawyer was both physically and mentally sharp. Michael Cooper was a well-dressed, articulate 42-year-old professional bull-shitter. His look was very studious, clean cut, and dapper. His clothes had Ralph Lauren written all over them and his shoes and tie always complimented his entire outfit. He was clean-shaven with a thin red mustache that he kept trimmed to perfection to match his neatly cut red hair. Definitely an Ivy League type of guy. He would constantly tell me and KK, "Don't worry about the case, let me do all of the worrying." Well the reality of it was we couldn't help but worry since we knew that KK was facing 10 to 20 years for possession of illegal drugs with intent to sell. Plus since we lived near a junior high school they added this new law that adds a mandatory five years for selling drugs in a school zone.

In court, Mr. Cooper had KK's case postponed three different times until the judge that he played golf with on a daily basis was available. He wanted to assure us a victory so he didn't take any chances on getting a judge that he didn't know personally.

The day of KK's trial both her and I were a bag of nerves. Between the two of us we probably had two hours of sleep, but Mr. Cooper put us at ease when we sat in court and watched as he sieged the entire courtroom.

"Your honor, before we even begin this case I would like to make you aware that not only is the DA not prepared to present his case, but the arresting officer is on an emergency vacation which I think is totally absurd."

The judge looked over at the D.A.

"Is this true council?" looking at him from over the top of his Benjamin Franklin style glasses.

"Well sort of your honor. Detective Smith took an emergency stress vacation for a month due to over exertion on the job."

Snatching off his glasses to reveal the bags under his eyes.

"Emergency vacation! "Don't I look like I need a vacation," the judge said abruptly.

The audience and jury all laughed, and in seeing that Mr. Cooper continued to antagonize the District Attorney.

"Your honor apparently the DA and the City of Philadelphia Police Department don't consider this case crucial enough to prosecute Mrs. Pizarro. Mrs. Pizarro, her son, and myself have been to this very courtroom three times to no avail, and the data they claim to have has been so severely tampered with that the evidence department and the arresting officers have different figures of the amount drugs and money that was supposed to be confiscated. I highly recommend that this case be thrown out due to negligence and impertinence by the police department."

The judge played right into it. Shuffling through his papers.

"Well Council, after carefully reviewing the evidence presented I don't see grounds to continue prolonging this case. In fact I don't see enough proof or evidence to pursue this case any longer. It's a waste of my time and taxpayer's money. Motion granted; case dismissed!"

Then he slammed his gavel and just like that it was over. The D.A. was so pissed off he stormed out of the courtroom. I didn't realize what had happened until Mr. Cooper suggested that we leave the courtroom right away.

"Let's take the back steps instead of the elevator just in case one of the arresting officers happen to show up late," Mr. Cooper insisted.

You should have seen the three of us flying down City Hall's spiral staircase. At the bottom of the stairwell, the three of us were out of breath. We both hugged and thanked Mr. Cooper.

" You two stay out of trouble for a while but if for some reason you just can't resist, you know how to reach me," with that million-dollar smile of his.

Mr. Cooper made a hefty $ 64,500 off of us but it was well worth KK not having to go to jail. KK and me both knew that she was supposed to be in jail with the amount of drugs and money they caught her with. I knew then she too had an angel.

The rest of the week I couldn't stop thinking about what the reverend said about being saved. I always believed there was a God but didn't know much about him. Since most of my friends were Muslim, I went to the Mosque a few times but never paid much attention to the speaker. I just went through the motions.

Also since most of my friends were drug dealers and drug users it all seemed a little phony to me going to make prayer with a kufi on your head on Friday and then going home, taking it off, and go back to selling drugs to the so called black man. I felt this urgent need to go back to the church where Case's funeral was.

That Saturday night Zack called me up to go out to the club.

"Naw man, I'm going to church tomorrow."

"Oh hell no! Now this nigga wants to be a preacher!"

"I'm not saying that I want to be a preacher but I don't know man, something happened to me at Case's funeral. It was a feeling that I can't describe. I don't even know what it was but I liked it and I'm going back for more."

" Man you sound like a fiend or something talkin about you "going back for more." Well I want some more too. Girls. Yea that's it. I want more girls."

"Well go and get all the girls you like. I'm going to church tomorrow."

"Man you're a nut."

He hung up the phone in my ear.

I had another homeboy from West Oak Lane named Bill. He would party with us sometimes but he was at church almost every Sunday. I knew he would go to church with me since I visited his church about two years ago before but promised I wouldn't go back. The day I visited Bill's church I will never forget.

First of all I don't know many church songs but the choir and members were singing songs that I've never heard in my life. Then came his pastor. He said that they were going to have church outside in the lawn a while back even though it was going to rain. Then he told everyone not only did it not rain that day but , **HE** made it not rain for two weeks. Then he called all of the prophets up to the front of the church which was around ten of them. (I didn't know I was surrounded by so many prophets). Then the prophets prayed for Bill and mugged him and told him to "Run for the Lord," he took off running. I mean he was doing laps around the church until he was exhausted. That was my last time at his church.

"Hell yeah I'll go to church with you. It's about time one of yawl boys saw the light. I mean don't get me wrong, I do my dirt too G but I give God his props every Sunday."
Then he got spiritual on me. "

G, Little do you know that feeling you felt at Case's funeral was the Holy Spirit working on your soul man. It's a beautiful feeling ain't it?"

"Yea man it did feel kind of good."

"G the lord is calling you man. He wants to save your soul, so don't sleep on it. Your one of his chosen ones."

I started to feel a little uneasy.

"Look, lets not jump to conclusions. I'm not saying that I'm going to be holier than thou but I do feel the need to go back."

"Then let's go."

Sunday morning I was as sharp as a tack. After breakfast, I put on my black, single-breasted Italian cut Armani suit. My pants had a 1/8-inch cuff to show off my black alligator boots with matching silk socks of course. Since I didn't want to wear a tie I decided to go with a cream cashmere, three-button pullover sweater to break up some of the black. I splashed on my favorite Lagerfeld cologne and dug deep down in my jewelry box for my gold cross KK had bought me when I was in the Corps to wear around my neck. When I looked in the mirror, I knew I was ready.

As I was leaving the building I heard KK call me.

"Giovanni you forgot something."

She ran to the door and handed me her bible, straightened out my lapel, and kissed my forehead.

"Now you're ready."

I smiled at her and headed to church.

At church before the sermon they asked all of the visitors to stand up so that they can be acknowledged. I was a little hesitant but after Bill stood up and I saw everyone was greeting him and shaking his hand praising God, I wanted to be acknowledged too. After all, I was the one wearing the Armani suit.

When the preacher spoke it felt as if he were speaking to me personally. He was saying how we do things in life that we know are wrong but we do them anyway and then feel guilty afterwards. He explained how everybody sins but Jesus died for all of the sins of the world and if you ask for forgiveness and repent, he will forgive your sins. Also, if you confess with your mouth and believe in your heart that Jesus Christ is Lord, you will be saved.

At the end of the sermon the preacher had an alter call for unsaved people to come up to the front of the church so he could pray for them and lead them to Christ. While Bill was praying I felt driven to approach the alter. Although my legs felt weak like linguini noodles, I excused myself to go past Bill and the other people in the pew so I could go up to the front of the church. I was nervous but my legs kept moving my body forward. "Praise God!, Hallelujah!, Hallelujah!," people were yelling as I walked down the center of the isle to the front of the church to receive my salvation. That day I accepted Christ. I looked back at Bill and smiled. As he was clapping along with everyone else, I could see his eyes restraining the tears.

Ch 21 The Truth Will Set You Free

I was a soldier for the Lord. I came home from church extremely excited telling my whole family about my salvation only to be knocked down by their criticism.

My family was sitting at the dining room table,

"I wish you would make up your mind about what you're going to be," Banita said. "When you were young you went to Catholic Church with your godmother like a good little alter boy. Then for the past few years you claim to be Muslim with your As-Salaamu-fake-um friends. You even went to the Kingdom Hall after you started dating a Jehovah's Witness girl. What's next, are you going to start saying, "Buddha bless you?"

Banita started laughing.

"I really crack myself up sometimes."

I didn't like her comment.

" Banita I know your atheist ass ain't talking because you never honored or stood for anything. And you know what they say. "If you don't stand for something, you'll fall for anything."

She stopped laughing.

" Oh yeah, well all of these years the whole family is convinced that you are just plain confused. And you know what they say, "If everybody is singing the same song, it's a hit."

At this point she was really starting to piss me off but I had to maintain my composure. After all, I just came from church.

"See what you don't understand is that this is different. I didn't call on the Lord, the Lord called on me. I'm just responding."

Banita's face changed instantly from happy to sad.

180

"Well I'm not saying that I don't believe in God but where was God when Case got killed? Or when Grandma died a slow agonizing death and she never did no wrong to anybody."

At that KK butted in.

"Alright Banita, that's enough. Leave your brother alone. I know personally that it was no one but God that saved me from going to jail so if he is saying that the Lord is calling him, then I think it's the right thing that he's doing by listening."

I was surprised but impressed. KK hardly ever got in the middle of our disagreements yet alone take my side. I guess the Lord was working on her too.

"Thanks mamma bear."

I kissed her on the cheek, stuck out my tongue at Banita like a little kid, and went upstairs to my apartment.

In my apartment I changed back into my street clothes and walked around the corner to Zack's house to tell him what happened to me at church but before I could share the news with him he cut me off.

" I don't know what's up with Jones, G acting all weird and strange and shit. His cousin Mook told me that he's broke. He said he blew all of his money on ho's. He said that he even lost his house and car because he couldn't keep up with the payments and had to move back to his mom and pop's house. I tried to call him a few times but his cell phone and pager are cut off and every time I call his mom's house they tell me that he's asleep or not home. I hope that he's not smoking that shit G."

"Naw Zack, Jones is far too smart for that. I'll swing by his crib on my way home and check on him."

At Jones house I finally found someone who was excited about my salvation.

"Praise the Lord," she said as Mrs. Jones hugged me. She seemed more excited then I was. She was an old, short, sweet, fat lady with a warm hug and a big heart.

"Giovanni, this is the best decision that you could have ever made. Now you are protected by the blood of Jesus."

"But Mrs. Jones, the funny thing is that I didn't make the decision, I guess the Lord did. He drew me to him. I don't know, I can't explain it."

"Well then that's even better. Now you can pray with us for Anthony, he's not feeling well. I told him that he drinks too much beer. I think it's his liver."

"Is he home?"

"Yeah baby he's in his room. Why don't you go on up there and tell him your good news," she said with a bright smile.

"Thank you Mrs. Jones."

I headed up the stairs to Jones room.

I knocked on the door and got no answer. After the third knock I turned the door knob, it was unlocked. I stuck my head in first then headed in.

Jones's room was a mess. It had depression written all over it. Piles of dirty clothes, empty beer cans, liquor bottles, and potato chip bags were scattered everywhere. It just wasn't like Jones to live like this. I was surprised that Mrs. Jones let him get away with keeping his room in the condition that it was in.

The room was dark with only a thin beam of sunlight coming through the crack of his window shade. It even smelled like he peed on himself. I nudged Jones shoulder with my hand.

"Dude, wake up." He was still half asleep.

"Who in the hell is in my room!"

Jones jumped up pissed off.

If These Streets Could Talk

"It's me man, get up! Whatcha gonna do sleep all day? You know don't nothing come to a sleeper but a dream," shaking him a little harder.

Jones sat up and reached over to his dresser and turned on his lamp. The low watt bulb didn't make the room much brighter. Squinting and rubbing his eyes trying to get them to focus.

"What in the hell are you doing here?" he said with a disgusted voice.

"I told my mom not to let **nobody** up here."

"Man you know those rules don't apply to me, I'm family," I said playfully punching him on his leg.

Then I got serious.

"Jones what's wrong with you man?"

He threw the covers over his head and rolled back over.

"Nothing, I just don't feel good."

I snatched his blanket from over his head.

"You don't feel good how?"

Jones reached over to his table lamp and put it up to his face. When I looked at him I was startled. He had discolored blotches all over his face and his skin was dry with a grayish undertone to it. His hair texture was different sort of thinner and curly and his cheek bones looked sunk in. Jones was a large boy and although he was lying down it was clear to see he was about 70 or 80 lbs lighter.

"What do you think is wrong with me," he said bitterly. "I hear the word on the street is that I'm smoking crack. Somebody else told me everyone is saying that I lost my mind. Well I'm here to tell you G that I got that hot shit."

Looking at him confused, "What hot shit?"

" The hivs, AIDS, HIV, the hot stuff."

I sat down on a pile of dirty clothes that was on his chair.

"Are you sure man? How do you know?"

Putting the lamp back up to his face.

"Does this shit look normal to you? I've been diagnosed with full-blown AIDS. The doctor said that if I would have caught it in its earlier stages they might have been able to control it some but it's too late now."

I sat back in the chair and thought about how I saw this coming. You see Jones was a nymphomaniac. A sex addict. I mean I too had a high sex drive but Jones was a little sick with his. He would go above and beyond the call of duty for sex. He would have sex three, four, sometimes even five times a day with different women, sometimes even crack-heads bragging how he was trying to break Wilt Chamberlain's so called 20,000 women record. He would also boast about not using condoms with this little rhyme he had…..

"I- make -sure- everything I hit is raw, I -make- sure- everything I hit is raw", indicating that he always has unprotected sex.

Jones had an extremely worried look on his face.

" G, Make sure that you get checked for this thing. I don't wish this shit on my worst enemy."

Then for the first time in our lives, I actually saw Jones cry.

"It hurts when I cough and my entire body is aching. I'm so weak that I can't even open a bottle of soda. I'm constantly pissing and shitting on myself. Man I wish I would just die."

My heart felt extra heavy for him. I wanted to embrace him but honestly I was afraid. I was ignorant to the fact that you couldn't catch AIDS by touching someone so I didn't want to get too close.

"You're going to be all right dude," was all that I could say to him from a distance. Then I felt the need to change the subject.

"Hey, guess what?"

He sat up in the bed whipping his tears away with his pajama sleeve.

"What."

"I got saved today."

Jones suddenly stopped crying and looked up at me.

"You did?"

"Yes I did and I know that you're saved and according to what the pastor showed us in the bible you can't loose your salvation, so Jones you're going to be all right because you are the righteousness of God man. And you know God says, "he'll never leave or forsake you." And you and I both know God **can't** lie."

Still wiping the tears from his eyes.

"G, can you do me a favor?"

Looking at him sympathetically.

"Anything my brotha.

He stretched his hands out towards me.

"Can you come down here and pray with me?" At that very moment I was no longer afraid of Jones's appearances. I knew he needed this and I had to do it for him. Even though I never actually prayed with anyone before I walked over to his bed, got on my knees, and took both of his hands in mine.

Me and Jones must have prayed for at least an hour asking God to forgive us for all of our sins and everything that we've done wrong to people in the past. We prayed for everyone else who had this crippling disease and we even prayed for a possible cure. I think we prayed for everything and everybody that day.

I visited Jones every day since our prayer marathon but about three weeks later the AIDS virus took total control over Jones's entire body and he died. At his funeral I didn't even cry. I knew that he was saved and at peace with the Lord and I would see him again in heaven some day. I had thought about my promiscuous past and made a mental note to myself that if I did have sex I would always use a condom and start making regular check ups to assure that I too hadn't contracted the AIDS virus.

I had a lot of built up guilt inside of me at Jones's funeral realizing that I was the one who introduced him to street life and how if I hadn't given him his first joint he might have been a professional sports player or something. But then I thought God had a plan for us all and everything happens for a reason.

If These Streets Could Talk

Ch 22 The Backslide

Although I received my salvation I was still allowing my sinful nature to override my spiritual nature. The only difference was that when I did something wrong I actually felt bad as opposed to when I wasn't saved and did awful things I actually enjoyed doing them.

Me and Yalanna were trying to patch up what little we had left of our relationship but I was still sneaking over to Coatesville seeing Marnissa. Even though she didn't possess the feminine characteristics that I like in women, I was still attracted to her ghetto beauty.

It was the summer of '92' and we had record-breaking heat. Me and KK never fully recovered financially after the robbery and court cost. In time I sold my other cars and only kept my XR4Ti. I always lived by the motto, "You got to pay to play," but my player status was the saddest with no money in my pockets.

Ania was almost a year old so I gave Marnissa my one and only air conditioner to keep her and the baby cool while I dealt with only having a fan in my apartment. That weekend was Marnissa's birthday so I decided to pop up over her house and surprise her with a bottle of champagne to celebrate. I lied to Yalanna telling her that I was swinging out with my boys for the evening and wouldn't be home until late.

When I reached Coatesville Projects I didn't want to look like I wasn't from the area so I put my diamond encrusted, name engraved necklace in my glove compartment. Then I put on my poker face as I walked past people standing around outside selling drugs, doing drugs, gambling, drinking, just doing a little bit of everything. Even though I'm from the hood I knew better then to draw any unnecessary attention to myself when I'm out of my element.

When I reached Marnissa's apartment I knocked on her door. It took Marnissa longer than normal to answer so I knocked harder.

When she opened the door and saw that it was me, her eyes lit up like two light bulbs. She was wearing a short pink robe and her hair was a mess. I glanced over at the couch and saw Ania there asleep, lying under a fan, sucking on a pacifier, sweating like a Hebrew slave.

"Why didn't you tell me you were coming G," she said trying to fix her hair and tie her robe.

"Because it's your birthday and I wanted to surprise you," allowing her to see the bottle of champagne I was holding in my hand as I suspiciously scanned my eyes around the entire room noticing an X-rated videotape on top of the VCR.

As sexual as Marnissa was, I knew that she didn't like watching porno tapes because I tried a couple of times to get her to watch one with me but she said that they just turned her off.

Still stalling me at the door not letting me in.

"G you should have called first."

At that point I got fed up.

"Alright let's cut through the shit! Why is my baby laying on that hot ass couch under a fan and you got the air on in your bedroom?"

She took a deep breath trying to compose herself. "Look G, don't trip but I got company ok."

Those words filled me with instant fury. I took a deep breath trying to calm myself down.

" Let me get this straight. You got company in your bedroom lying under **my** air-conditioner while my daughter is lying on the couch sweating bullets. Bitch you must have lost your dam mind!"

Just then some dude came out of the bedroom with only a pair of jeans on exposing his Jockey Boxer shorts and was wearing no shirt or shoes. I immediately sized him up. He was about 6ft tall, 170 to 180 lbs. He also had a very muscular toned body filled with tattoos that weren't very visible because of his extremely dark skin.

Scratching his nappy bushy hair, "Yo man, ya'll got's to keep it down up in here while a nigga is tryin to get his sleep on," he said as he walked into the kitchen opening the refrigerator door leaning down looking inside.

Case taught me to never fight over a woman nor never get into a confrontation with another man if you catch your woman cheating. After all, it's her fault not his. A man is going to be a man. Plus Marnissa wasn't really my woman. She was just the mother of my child who I was sleeping with on a regular basis.

Well I don't know if I was more upset at the fact that Marnissa had just screwed another man while my baby was on the couch or the fact that this dude was lying under my air conditioner and getting funky with me, but at that point it didn't even matter. Marnissa tried to grab my arm as I darted into her apartment but I yanked away from her grip and headed over towards the refrigerator. The dude was still bending over scrambling around inside the refrigerator.

" Yo Niss, you got some lunchmeat or something up in here? I'm as hungry as a hostage."

When he stood up to close the refrigerator door all he could do was open his mouth in disbelief as he saw the champagne bottle in my hand raised high in the air. "CRACK." I busted the bottle of Champagne over his head as he hit the floor like a falling tree. Marnissa was standing behind me and before I knew it I hit her with a right cross to her head sending her into the wall then hitting the floor hard.

"Why did you hit me?", she moaned holding the side of her face while lying on the floor exposing her nakedness from under the robe.

I stood over her.

"You figure it out you little trick."

At that point Ania woke up crying so while the big black buck was out on the floor unconscious I hurried into the bedroom and gathered up whatever clothing I seen that belonged to my baby. I then snatched my air-conditioner from out of the window, wrapped Ania up in a blanket, and rushed out of the apartment. I knew I had to get out of the projects before Marnissa's comatose boyfriend woke up and called his posse on me. The whole time Marnissa didn't say anything. She just lay on the floor holding the side of her face crying feeling stupid and embarrassed.

I jumped in my car and hit I95 as fast as I could hoping Marnissa didn't call the police on me for kidnapping my daughter.

Case always said the first step in eliminating a relationship is to eliminating the bed and he was right. You can't sleep with a person on a daily basis and not expect to catch some kind of feelings.

After that day I vowed to never sleep with Marnissa again and I didn't. She was too high risk. High risk disease, high risk pregnancy, high risk trouble. Just plain high risk.

Now here I was a twenty seven year old ex-drug dealer with only a car, an apartment, a newborn baby, and limited funds. I hated the thought of it, but the reality was I had to get a job.

A friend of KK's who was one of our old customers got me a job at a hospital in West Philly as a dietary aide serving and preparing food for patients. I hadn't had a legal job in years so the whole thing was like a new experience to me. At that time, KK became my built in babysitter. Whenever I had to work she would watch Ania for me. I tried to pay her but she wouldn't take any money." How can I charge you for watching my granddaughter? " She would constantly say.

I would have to actually sneak money into her purse when she wasn't looking so I wouldn't feel guilty.

My first day on the new job my stomach was bubbling inside from the cookies and milk I had eaten the night before. Even though I'm lactose intolerant I could never resist some Chips Ahoy Cookies and a glass of ice-cold milk before bed. I was just accustomed to suffering the consequences in the morning.

I couldn't hold it any longer so I went to the bathroom during my first break to relieve myself. I never really felt comfortable using public restrooms, but my stomach said "NOW!"

After leaving the bathroom I walked back to my training area and noticed a few people looking at me strangely. Then it appeared to me that a few people were even laughing at me until finally this older guy came over to me.

"I see where you've been," pointing at my butt. I turned my head around to look at the back on my pants and seen a long piece of toilet paper coming out the top of my belt area all the way down to the ground. You see whenever I have to use a public toilet, I coat the toilet seat with about a half of roll of toilet paper and I must have gotten some caught in my pants when I pulled them up. Then to make things look even more disgusting, the tip of the piece of toilet paper that was coming out of my pants was wet. I had never been so embarrassed in my entire life. Needless to say my first week at work everybody called me, "Shitty".

Working at the hospital was pretty cool. I liked the people, I liked the work, but I didn't like the pay. Going from $2,000 a day to $9.00 an hour was financially traumatizing. Even though Ania lived with me, Marnissa resented me so much that she had the nerve to take me to child support court allowing them to deduct $200 a month out of my check leaving me with peanuts to live off of. I didn't fight it in court because all I wanted was my Ania to stay with me.

Making this slow money drove me crazy. When I went shopping I would have to buy Ania clothes and pampers instead of spending everything on myself like I was used to doing. I couldn't sell any more weed since I knew the cops were watching me and KK after she avoided going to jail. I knew there had to be some way to make some side cash at the hospital since there were so many people. It was time to do my homework.

I met this guy named George who worked in housekeeping. In time I found out he was also the hospital loan shark. He was a sort of frail light skinned guy about 45 years old who had been working at the hospital for about fifteen years so he pretty much knew everybody. He would loan people money until the following payday at the rate of fifty cents on a dollar. In other words, if you barrow $50 from him, on payday you would pay back $75. If you borrow $100 you would have to pay back $150 and so on. He was getting rich turning money into money and I wanted in.

I slowly got close to George to learn his business and watch who his customers were. In time I learned that he had the entire hospital on his payroll. Environmental Service, Dietary, Security, Distribution. He even had some Nurses and Nursing Assistants on his list. Some people who borrowed money just needed a few dollars to get by until payday since we got paid every other week but I noticed that most of his people used the money to buy drugs.

George was all right but he was soft. He kept his fingernails filed to perfection and he wore clear fingernail polish on them like he was a pimp or something. Any man that gives his fingernails that much attention is definitely suspect in my book.

If These Streets Could Talk

People would come to George short of what they owed him and he would let them get away with it. Case always said, "If you have a friend that you want to get rid of, loan him some money because you'll never get it back," and he was right. Some people would even duck George on payday to avoid paying him at all. He didn't even worry or look for them. He would let them get away with it.

"G I don't sweat them because I'm getting paid anyway so I just turn the other cheek and keep gettin' my money."

Wrong answer! The amount of money isn't the point, the fact that they owe you money is the principal. On the streets you can't just turn the other cheek because you'll get slapped on the other side of your face. When I saw how weak George was I decided to start a little loan shark business of my own.

I started telling a few of George's customers that if they needed to borrow any money that they could come and see me. I slowly started stealing George's customers right from under his nose. People that owed him money who didn't plan on paying him bought their business to me but the difference was I gave them all the same speech.

"I'm not George so don't ever try to screw me. I tell you one time and one time only. I don't take no shorts."

Everything was going well until a few weeks later when I was alone in the locker room one afternoon changing into my street clothes after finishing my shift. When I looked up while tying my sneakers George walked in closing then locking the door behind him. I wasn't intimidated at all but I didn't know how he was going to approach me so I stood up so I wouldn't be in a vulnerable position. Case always taught me to never underestimate anybody. Cowards even sometimes show heart when their backs are against the wall.

George slowly walked towards me.

"I hear you got a little loan shark business going on for yourself."

I figured there was no use lying since everyone knew what I was doing.

"Well you sure got good ears because you heard right," I replied in a boastful manner.

Then came his tough guy approach. He pulled out a pair of brass knuckles and slid them on his hand and continued slowly walking towards me.

" George, I think you better pump your brakes and think about what you're doing."

"Oh yeah, well I already thought about it young boy. I started this loan shark business and I'd be damned if I'm going to let some little ass, has been, drug dealer come in and interfere with my operation."

I looked at him surprised that he knew about the "W".

"Yeah that's right, I know all about you on the so called "W" Mr. Big time weed man. Now look at you. Passing out food trays to old sick people smelling like fried chicken. You went from riches to rags and now you think that you can just come up in here and take things over? Well it ain't gonna happen Captain," he said pressing his finger on my nose. "You better shut your mouth and sit down or I will, you snotty nose little punk."

Case always said never pull out a weapon unless you're ready to use it. Case also taught me to never fear the weapon but the man behind the weapon and I sure as hell wasn't afraid of George. He also taught me that the best fight is the one where you don't get hit so it was time to react.

If These Streets Could Talk

Before George could blink I kneed him directly between his legs so hard that the both of us fell. I immediately got up and stood over him looking down at him.

"If you really know so much about me then you would have known not to come off like a fake ass gangster if you really ain't one."

While he was on his hands and knees gasping for air after the old knee to the balls technique, I kicked him in his mouth sending him flat on his back.

"Now I'm going to show you how to really be gangster."

I leaned over and pulled him up by is collar.

" From here on out your business is officially closed down. If I hear about you even loaning out one dollar I'll sick my dogs on you and have them beat you down until you're unrecognizable!"

I threw him on his back and gave him a stomp to the middle of his stomach forcing him to ball up in a fetal position. Then I reached down checking all of his pockets and took all of his money which was about $1000. I left him lying on the ground moaning as I walked away.

I actually felt bad dogging George like I did but I needed his business and he was weak enough to take it. Case always taught me, survival of the fittest. The strong out power the weak. "Only the strong survive."

If These Streets Could Talk

Ch 23 Just Say No

I felt like I was back on the map. This loan shark thing was sweet. After extorting George for his business he ended up quitting his job at the hospital leaving me with a fairly profitable business. I began loaning out $1,000 to $1,500 every pay period making $500 to $750 profit just turning money into money.

At first a few people were trying to short me from time to time like they did George but after I gave Zack a few dollars to come down to the hospital and slap around, beat down, and choke a few folks, the word got around the hospital to have all of my money right on time, every time.

While at the hospital I met this pretty little Puerto Rican nurse named Abigail who would borrow money from me from time to time. And although she was a nurse, she was a little silly. I think she liked me because I always made her laugh. She was always giggling at every little joke I would tell. Real smart girl but lacked common sense. She had more degrees than a thermometer but less cents than a nickel. But what she lacked in brains she sure as hell made up in beauty. She was thirty years old, short with light brown skin and long thick curly black hair that came down to the middle of her back. Gorgeous! Like I said most of my customers were drug users or abusers and in time I found out that she was both.

On one occasion, Abigail called me and asked if she could borrow $100 and if I could come over to her apartment and bring it to her. Normally I wouldn't make house calls but I was always a sucker for beauty so I agreed to deliver the cash.

The inside of Abugail's apartment was very neat and clean with a lot of live plants and scented candles everywhere. I knew her rent was high since her high rise was located in Center City so I assumed she got paid well for being a nurse.

"Why don't you have a seat and make yourself comfortable while I take a quick shower," pouring me a drink of cognac on the rocks and then going into the bathroom.

As I sat on her plush couch sipping on my drink, I glanced around the room noticing hangings on her walls in addition to her expensive paintings were all sort of nursing certificates and awards she had acquired over the years. I also noticed that she had a very expensive crystal and lie leek collection in a beautiful glass curio.

As I reached for the remote control that was sitting on the coffee table in front of me I noticed a small bag of cocaine and a straw sitting on the table. It turned me off instantly. As fine as Abigail was the thought of her snorting cocaine made me lose all interest since I knew first hand what cocaine does to people.

Abigail got out of the shower and came back into the living room with one towel rapped around her body and another rapped around her head.

"I didn't know you did that stuff," I said pointing at the bag of white powder sitting on the table.

" Oh don't sweat that Popi I only do it occasionally. Sometimes I have to work long hours and it helps to keep me awake," she said with that sexy Spanish accent.

"Well did you ever consider drinking coffee or taking No-Dose instead?"

"You so silly Papi, "she said as she plopped down next to me on the couch.

"Why, don't you get down?" offering me the bag of coke.

"Nope, never touched the stuff," pushing the bag on the table further away from me.

"I've seen too many of my people go crazy over that shit."

She stood up and removed the towel from around her head allowing her silky wet hair to fall down her caramel colored back, shaking her head from side to side.

"Do I look crazy to you?," she said as she removed the second towel from around her body allowing me to see the rest of her nakedness.

My heart skipped a beat. Her sexy and flawless body had me mesmerized. She took my drink from my hand and sat it on the coffee table then took me by the hand and led me into her bedroom. I'll let you figure out the rest.

Afterwards we showered together and she cooked some chicken with beans and yellow rice, which was right in my Latino blood. I learned from my Spanish side of the family that most Puerto Ricans know how to throw down in the kitchen.

Then it happened. She got a razor blade from out of the bathroom, went over to the coffee table, and started to chop away at the cocaine that she had in the small bag on the table. I watched as she divided it up in thin lines. Since her hair was so long she slung it all to one side and snorted the substance through her straw, first in one nostril then in the other. Handing me the straw. "Here Papi just try it and if you don't like it just leave it alone."

After the love making session I just experienced with Abigail I probably would have tried some heroin if she had offered it me to so I took the straw and snorted one line of coke in one nostril then one in the other and sat up.

"I don't see what all the hype is about." I handed her back the straw.

Then for the next sixty seconds I felt my nostrils slowly become numb. The gradual freeze felt a little wired but kind of good almost like a shot of Novocain wearing off after leaving a dentist office.

She could tell by the look on my face that the cocaine was taking affect.

"See, I told you," she said smiling. "It's nice ain't it?"

Trying to be cool, "Yeah, it's kind of smooth." I took another sip of my Hennessey while enjoying my frozen nostrils.

We sat at that table snorting the coke until the whole bag was gone. Needless to say I ended up giving her the $100 instead of loaning it to her. This was the beginning of a major mistake.

If These Streets Could Talk

Ch 24 Used And Abused

With my newfound girlfriend and newfound high I felt like a new man. One Saturday night, Gail wanted to go to Atlantic City to see Teena Marie live so I charged us some tickets.

We both put on our sharpest gear and bought plenty of nose candy for our drive to AC. We talked, laughed, snorted, and listened to music all the way to Atlantic City looking forward to seeing my favorite singer of all time. Is it me or did Tina Marie never really get her props? Her voice was definitely a gift from God.

As soon as we walked into Trump Plaza, Gail's eyes lit up checking out all of the high rollers, money, and lights everywhere. Immediately grabbing my hand, she said, "Come on Papi, let's play some craps. Give me some money Baby," she said looking as if she had drool coming from out of the side of her mouth.

I had about $3,000 dollars on me so I counted out five one hundred dollar bills and put them in her hand.

"Take it easy Gail, that's all I'm giving you so make it last"

She threw the five Benjamin's on the crap table in exchange for chips.

I watched my $500 disappear in approximately two minutes.

"This is bullshit!" she said when she lost her last chip. Holding her hand out for me to give her some more money "let me try again Popi."

I pushed her hand away, "Slow down bad luck Slep Rock. You chill out for a while and let me try my luck."

I stood near the table and examined how the game was played. It was similar to street craps but Atlantic City gives you plenty more options. I watched for about thirty minuets until I got a better understanding of what was going on.When I felt comfortable enough to play, I threw $500 on the table in exchange for chips.

When the dice reached me I threw $300 worth of chips on the table. My first number was a six. I stacked the dice on top of each other like I would on the streets and threw two threes right back.

"Get em Papi!"

Gail picked up my winnings jumping up and down for joy.

After that I was on a roll hitting every number on the dice. People surrounded our table betting on any and every number I threw. I must have stayed on the dice for about forty-five minutes before finally crapping out.

That evening my total winnings was $14,600 so the hotel gave me and Gail a honeymoon suite on the house.

We felt like high rollers but little did we know all of the hotels in AC and Las Vegas do that when you win big to keep you there so you won't leave with the money. They've been running that scheme for years on people and it worked.

We went to the concert, made love, snorted coke, and drank all night until we both passed out.

The following night after dinner we went shopping at the Gucci shop and hit the craps table again in hopes of another big win except this time I couldn't hit any number on the dice.

By the end of the evening, we had lost all of the money we had left after shopping.

After that, me and Gail were going down Atlantic City every weekend trying to win big again but it never happened. What people don't realize is that AC and Las Vegas is not designed for you to win. If it were, there would be no AC or Vegas.

Between our coke habit and gambling habit, in a matter of weeks my savings account dwindled down to nothing. Gail had me spending so much money that even my loan shark business was finished since I didn't have the money to loan out anymore.

Then a few weeks later after I was dead broke and back to making $9.00/hr, Gail told me that we shouldn't see each other anymore. She actually told me that she was too high maintenance for me and that I couldn't afford her. How typical?

At first I considered setting her apartment on fire but my conscious wouldn't let me do it, so instead I did a little trick that Case taught me to drive a person crazy.

When I went to Gail's apartment to pick up the rest of my belongings that she had boxed up, while she was in her bedroom, I took five raw jumbo shrimp I had in some foil in my pocket. I took out my pocket knife and cut open the top hem of her living room curtain and slid the raw shrimp in it. You see, after a few days when the shrimp start to smell they give off an odor that could kill a horse. A person goes crazy trying to find out where the smell is coming from. I felt as though I at least owed her that.

Then one week after our break up rumor had it that Gail started dating a doctor at the job. Little Puta! I felt like a first class sucker letting Gail bring me back down to the gutter and not even realizing she was only using me for my money. I really thought I was a player until I got played.

Later that evening I snuck into the employee parking-lot at the hospital and flattened two of Gail's tires on her Jeep. Case said never flatten all four because they can file an insurance claim. Two is out of pocket. I admit it was a little petty but it gave me some sort of satisfaction. Case always said two wrongs don't make a right, but it damn sure makes it even.

My experience with Gail sure taught me one thing about cocaine. You can have a father, mother, child, job, house, car, or anything. But when you're hooked, it supersedes any and everything that may seem important in your life. No matter how much you try to get ahead, it retards your progress.

I had to think of a way to get back on my feet but little did I know, I had just stepped into quicksand.

If These Streets Could Talk

Ch 25 The IRS

Although Yalanna was devastated over me having a daughter by Marnissa she still stayed in my corner. She showed me how to change Ania's pampers, warm up milk, clean bottles and everything else that involved taking care of a baby. In a matter of a few weeks she turned me into Mr. Mom.

Three months had gone by and I hadn't heard a word from Marnissa. When I last called, her sister told me that she and the guy whose head I cracked opened at her apartment were engaged to get married. I think she was trying to make me jealous but I actually felt sorry for the guy. Doesn't he know you can't turn a ho into a housewife.

A few weeks later, I got a letter from the IRS for me to report to them with proof of income of everyone living in my household. In other words I got audited. You see for the last two years I had been claiming Maria's two oldest children on my income taxes to receive a larger refund check. In other words I was committing tax fraud. I couldn't believe it. Out of everyone I knew who cheated on his or her income taxes every single year, I would be the one to get audited.

The day came for my hearing. When I walked into the Federal Building I was relieved to see that I recognized the receptionist. It was this girl named Cheryl that used to buy weed from us and always ask to go out with me. I never dated her because she was about 100 lbs heaver than me but I felt sort of relieved when I saw her face. I thought, "Maybe she could pull some strings and help me get out of this audit."

"What's up Cheryl?"

Trying to look like I was thrilled to see her. "Long time no see."

She looked up, "Hey G baby what's up? Uh oh, don't tell me that you got audited," with a worried look on her face.

" Yea that's what I'm here for. Can you help a brother out?"

"Let me punch your name in the computer and see if I can get one of my girlfriends to handle your case."

As she pecked away at her keyboard I hung around her desk making small conversation hoping she could get someone that she knew to handle my case.

Just then a very stern looking middle age medium build black lady came through the door holding some papers in her hand. She looked like one of my Marine Corps drill instructors.

"Uh oh, G, that's my supervisor, good luck."

Then she spun back around in her chair shuffling around at her papers trying to look busy as if she didn't even know me.

"Giovanni Pizarro," the mean looking lady announced motioning for me to follow her.

As I followed her and looked back at Cheryl, she gave me the "Don't tell her where you know me from" look. I just walked behind her to her office with a bad feeling.

In her office, on her desk, was her name Marcia Banks. I tried to break the ice by respectfully referring to her by her last name.

"Mrs. Banks, can I explain what this is all about? I…

She rudely interrupted.

"Mr. Pizarro, I'll be asking you a series of five yes or no questions. If you answer any of the questions no, then you fail. Is that clear"?

"Yes, I guess."

I sat straight up in my chair.

I tried to catch eye contact with her hoping to dazzle her with my gift of charm but she didn't even look at me. She concentrated fully on the paperwork she had on the desk in front of her.

She began.

"In the years 1989 and 1990 did William and Robert Pizarro reside with you?"

I thought for a second this is going to be easy since I knew my two nephews did live with me and I could prove it since Maria's mail came to my house that year with their names on it.

"Yes they did," I said with sheer confidence and almost arrogance handing her a letter from the school district with both the boy's names on it addressed to my house.

She took the letter, looked at it briefly and handed it back to me looking somewhat disappointed.

"Alright Mr. Pizarro. In 1989 and 1990 did you provide medical coverage for William and Robert and if so, do you have documentation to prove it?"

Question number two was as far as I got .The game was over. I tried to stall as I looked through my folder for something but knew there was nothing to find. I looked up at her disappointingly.

"No they weren't."

When I said that, for the first time during our conversation, she looked up at me as if she were pleased to hear me say no.

"Well then Mr. Pizarro, you fail!"

She reached into the top drawer of her desk, pulled out a calculator, and went to work.

As her fingers attacked the calculator I didn't know if she was adding or multiplying but I felt like I was being finger whipped.

When she finally finished abusing the calculator buttons she spun it in my direction allowing me to see screen and sarcastically said,

"Mr. Pizarro, since you failed to provide proof of guardianship for your nephews for the past two years that you claimed them, you owe the IRS $8,600."

I was devastated. I just knew I was going to jail for tax fraud. I tried to plead my case.

"Mrs. Banks, I don't have $8,600 and the only way I can get it is if I hit the number and I don't see any lottery machines around here."

Still having that devilish grin on her face she just turned and said, "Well if you can't pay the balance due, you can set up a payment arrangement."

Payment arrangement? Is she kidding me? When you make $9.00/hr. and pay child support, payment arrangements aren't an option. I didn't know what I was going to do. Times were defiantly hard on the Boulevard and I didn't see any light at the end of the tunnel.

If These Streets Could Talk

Ch 26 A Child Is Born

Maria was so strung out on crack that she just abandoned her five kids on KK. Our apartment building was in need of necessary repairs and KK didn't have the money to make them. I also couldn't believe KK was doing domestic work cleaning doctors and lawyers houses again barely bringing in enough money to take care of herself but I guess when your back is against the wall, you do what you have to do.

Although me and Yalanna weren't together I would still on occasion spend the night at her apartment. Then one day she said those dreadful words that I had heard many times before.

"G, I'm pregnant."

I wasn't upset since the two of us had been down this road before. She made it simple and clear to just give her the money and she'll take care of the rest.

The following week Yalanna's mother went with her to the abortion clinic since I had to work.

When I came home from work Yalanna was sitting on my pouch with her eyes full of tears. I knew she had just had an abortion so I tried to be sympathetic. When I walked up to her to hug her she pushed me away.

"Don't touch me," she said while handing me a white envelope.

"What's this?" I opened it up.

"It's your money. I couldn't go through with it."

I thought to myself this was deja vu all over again. All I could say was, "Oh hell no! You got to do this; I can't afford any more kids. Ania is killing my pockets and I can't afford another baby!"

"Well you should have thought about that when you wasn't using a condom." I killed one child for you and I'm not doing it again. The same way you take care of Ania will be the same way you'll take care of this baby."

I just stood there with the stupid look on my face in disbelief as she walked away. I was miserable.

The next seven months were a living hell. Yalanna ran me non-stop. Every time she craved anything I had to go to the store and get it. We were back and forth at the doctor's for any and every discomfort that she felt. She even made me go to Lamaze classes with her once a week.

July 1, 1993. The day finally came when her water broke. I was totally prepared. I had her hospital bag packed and ready. I even had an overnight bag packed for myself since she made it very clear that I was going to be the coach during childbirth so I was ready with ice chips in hand (learned that in lamaze class).

In the delivery room I was impressed to see that the doctor was a thirty something year old black woman who had determined that Yalanna was not dilating enough so she had to perform an emergency cesarean.

I had heard of people getting C-sections but didn't know the extent of it.

Ok, I was not ready for a C-section. I spent four months in Lamaze classes preparing for natural child birth with ice chips, hand holding, forehead wiping, you know, coach stuff. This was totally different.

One of the doctor's assistants gave me a gown and mask just like they were wearing and told me to wash my hands thoroughly. Yalanna was on the operating table with a curtain the lower half of her body is covered during a c-section and enabling her to see her body from the waist down. She was only wearing a sheet and hairnet.

Once the procedure began it looked like everyone in the operating room was holding a piece of Yalanna's insides. I had never seen so much blood and guts in my entire life. One person was holding her intestines while someone else had her uterus and some other stuff. During the entire time the anesthesiologist was explaining the whole procedure to me as I was trying to keep my composure not knowing which was going to come first: the baby, me passing out, or me vomiting.

"You don't feel any of this?" I asked her still feeling nauseous.

"I don't feel any pain but I feel the pressure," she said as her body was moving from side to side as the doctor continued to gut her like a fish.

" Giovoni I feel something," Yalanna squeezed my hand harder. " I feel something ," I grunted as my lightheaded condition got worse.

After the doctor finally finished pulling out the uterus and everything else that's associated with delivering a baby, out came my son. I was astonished. It's amazing how God made women's bodies so perfectly to reproduce. My son was the most beautiful, stunning, handsome, wet, bloody, disgusting, chocolate little thing that I had ever seen in my entire life.

As soon as the doctor delivered him, she wiped him off then she gently placed him in my nervous hands and just like with Ania, I instantly fell in love.

If These Streets Could Talk

Ch 27 Four Wheels Beat Heels

After Jamere was born, me, Zack and my boy Shawn from down North Philly got together and starting buying and selling used cars at the auction. We all put a few hundred dollars upfront and would buy a squatter (an old used car) and sell it for double or triple of what we paid for it. We would take it home, shine it up inside and out, steam clean the engine, and throw a for sale sign on it. Then with our profit, we would buy two more and so on and so on. Soon we had squatters all over West Philly with our company logo name on them, "4 Wheels". Our motto was "4 wheels beat heels." It was a little corny but catchy.

One thing we learned quickly in the car selling business. Was when dealing with the public there are always problems. Some people would come to us asking for their money back complaining about problems that they were experiencing with the cars they purchased from us. That's when we came up with a three day, as is contract for people to sign whenever they bought a car. That way we were protected.

Once we sold a car to this young lady at my job and after the fourth day the engine froze. I mean the car wasn't doing anything at all. We were all standing outside on the "W" when I told Zack and Shawn, "We have to return this girl's money to her. She's a nice young lady with two kids and she purchased the car from us with her income tax money, so I don't want to rip her off like that."

"Man I don't care if she bought it with her kids college fund money, she gets nothing back, you know the rules," Zack said callously.

Shawn agreed.

"G three days is three days. She got the contract and that's the rules. She just got to bite the bullet and take the loss."

I started to get mad since no one was trying to hear what I was saying.

"Man I got to see this girl everyday at work knowing we sold her a car that was a lemon. Plus we only paid $250 for the Riviera and sold it for $1,000. Even if we give her half back we still wouldn't be taking a loss."

Zack came up close to my face.

"Read my lips G. The bitch gets nothing back!" he yelled in my face.

Before I knew it I mugged him hard in his face and it was on. He retaliated with a vicious left to my face and a right to my body forcing my knees to buckle. Shawn jumped in and grabbed him while I was on my knees trying to collect myself after totally getting the wind knocked out of me.

"What's wrong with yaw fools fighting over a car! We're supposed to be better than that."

"G if you ever put your hands in my face again, I will kill you," Zack threatened as Shawn continued to restrain him.

Shawn spun Zack around to where his back was facing me. Shawn tried to calm Zack down and explain to Zack how wrong he was for two piecing me. The whole time Shawn saw me creeping up behind Zack picking up a metal trashcan that was on the corner while still distracting Zack.

I crept up behind him

"CRASH".

I hit him in the back of his head so hard that the trashcan had the indentation of his skull in it. Shawn let him go and he dropped.

When he hit the ground I continued hitting him with the can until he could no longer attempt to stand to his feet because I knew if he could, he would kill me. Then Shawn grabbed me.

"Alright G that's enough, it's over."

Afterwards I apologized to Zack.

" It's cool G but you know if you wasn't my boy I would have killed you."

"Yeah, I know Zack. One love man." We hugged and bought a 40 oz. of beer and laughed about our little bout. He blacked my eye pretty badly but I definitely **trashed** him. We also agreed to end our business since it was jeopardizing our friendship so needless to say, "4 Wheels" was over.

If These Streets Could Talk

CH 28 Unbelievable

     I was at work the following week and got a message to call home immediately. When I called, Banita answered the phone.

     "G you got to come home right away. The building caught on fire."

     I dropped the phone and ran to my car. I heard my supervisor yell out, "Where in the hell do you think you're going?" I just ignored him and ran to my car.

     When I got to the "W" I was in shock. The building wasn't on fire, it was just my apartment on the third floor that was ablaze. It looked like something out of a movie. Fire was coming out of every window in my apartment. KK and the rest of the family were outside watching as the firemen extinguished the blaze.

     "Why is my apartment burnt to a crisp? " I asked as I ran up to KK.

     "I don't know. The kids said that they seen Maria sneak out of the building but I don't know. I haven't seen her in days."

     When the firemen left the scene, License and Inspection came in right behind them and told us the building had to be shut down right away due to extensive fire and water damage. They gave us a few hours to gather up all of our belongings and evacuate the building immediately.

     After we gathered all that we could carry, L&I boarded up all of the windows and doors then put orange abandon property stickers all around the building. They also warned us not to attempt to go back into the building until we fix everything up to code or we will be arrested.

     I lost everything I owned. I also found out KK didn't have any fire insurance on the building which meant it was a total loss. Luckily, I owned another house a few blocks away right off of 55th & Ceder Ave.

that I had inherited from my aunt so needless to say I put my tenets out and we all moved in: Me, Ania, KK, Banita, and Maria's five kids. We were one big miserable family.

In a matter of two weeks Maria's kids had managed to destroy my entire house. I'm talking holes in the walls, T.V and microwave broken, crayon marks everywhere. Everything made out of glass was broken including all of my dishes, my kitchen table and bathroom mirrors. I would come home from work every day and find something else destroyed. When I would ask who was responsible no one would confess. I think they had some kind of code of silence or something so I would give all five of them a beating together.

I came home from work and in my mailbox was a subpoena. Apparently Marnissa was taking me to court to regain custody of Ania. I couldn't believe it. I called her immediately.

"What's up with this subpoena?"

"What do you mean what's up with it. It is what it is, I'm taking your ass to court. Ania needs to be with me right now because you got too many people living in your nasty ass house and she doesn't need to be around those fresh ass nieces and nephews of yours. Plus I'm married now so you won't have a foot to stand on in court."

"Married? Who in their right mind would marry you? What's he on, dope or dog food?"

"Don't you worry about it. Let's see your face in court when Ania leaves with me."

Her saying that really pissed me off.

"Marnissa"

I tried to tell her coolly.

"I've had Ania for the past three and a half years without any help or support from you or your family. If you try to take her from me I promise to make you regret you ever knew me."

"Excuse me, are you threatening me? Don't make me bring my brothers over there and turn shit out."

Her threatening me really pissed me off.

" Your brothers would rather walk through a lion's den with pork chop drawers then come to the "W" looking for me. Now I'm telling you that if you love your brothers, please don't bring them over here because you won't ever see them again. Now do you want to try me?"

The phone was silent.

"Oh now you're crickets. I thought so."

"I hate you, you bastard! I'll see you in court!"

She slammed the phone in my ear.

For the next few weeks, I tried to prepare Ania for our court date but there was no preparation for our possible separation. She cried all the way to court that morning. Although she was only three years old, she was very bright and aware of what was going on. Little did she know while she was crying on the outside, I was crying on the inside.

In court Marnissa was right. I didn't have a leg to stand on. Marnissa's entire family was there in the courtroom giving me the evil eye the whole time. Marnissa and her husband stood at the podium together holding hands looking like the perfect couple.

When Marnissa spoke to the judge she completely bashed me describing every gory detail of my living conditions.

"Judge you should see the house that they live in. Holes in the walls. Dirty smelly clothes everywhere. They even have rats and roaches."

The lady judge looked at me astonished.

"Is that true Mr. Pizarro?"

It was embarrassing to even answer that question, but I had to pull out my courtroom face.

"First of all your honor, I don't have rats. Secondly, I am presently experiencing a family hardship and my overcrowded living condition is only temporary. I'm doing the best I can do right now under the present circumstances."

"Well Mr. Pizarro, sometimes our best just isn't good enough," she said coldly.

She shuffled through her papers then stated, "The court grants Mr. and Mrs. Mc Cloud residential custody and Mr. Pizarro visitation rights every other weekend. Mr Pizarro's child support payments are also to resume."

She slammed her gavel and just like that it was over. Marnissa rushed over to pick up Ania who was kicking and crying profusely.

"I want my daddy, I want my daddy!" Her voice echoed throughout the courtroom. I ran over towards Ania with my eyes full of tears but the two bailiffs restrained me. "Don't worry Sweetie, Daddy will be back to get you real soon!"

Then Marnissa started yelling at Ania.

"Shut up all of that noise! You'll see him again."

Then she looked back at me with a sarcastic look and fiendish grin.

" I told you I would win," she said as she stormed out of the courtroom with her family and my baby. I stood and watched as she left the courtroom with my baby. It took everything in me to hold back the tears but I refused to let Marnissa see me cry. I wouldn't give her the pleasure.

I knew I didn't have the best of living conditions but a real mother or father would <u>never</u> abandon their child under any circumstances the way Marnissa did. Ania was the only thing I had in my life that wasn't tainted, the only thing I had in my life that was pure and Marnissa knew it and used her as a tool to get to me. She could have gone about the situation in a different manner but her mission was to hurt me and she accomplished it. She vindictively broke my heart taking the one thing I loved more than myself. For the past three and a half years I dedicated my life to taking care of Ania and for the first time I felt as if I failed her.

After loosing custody of Ania I went into a deep depression. I've been stressed out before but never like this. It felt like the weight of the world was on my shoulders and my knees were giving out. I even contemplated suicide but the thought of leaving my children fatherless would not allow me to do it. Then I convinced myself that I had to be strong so I could get my daughter back.

Back at work we had a hospital wide meeting for all of the service departments. There were about 100 of us stuffed in one room when the president of the hospital came into the conference room with a worried look on his face. He approached the podium speaking softly into the microphone.

"Good afternoon everyone," clearing his throat.

" I may as well get straight to the point. I'm sorry to inform you all that we are experiencing major financial debt and it puts me in an awkward position but a mandatory hospital layoff will take affect immediately."

An abrupt outburst filled the room. Then someone yelled out,

"Everybody calm down and let him finish!"

He continued.

"The union agreed to do this according to seniority so we'll have to start from the newest hires to the last and work our way down."

Everyone in the room was astonished. This was a major bomb being dropped on all of us.

If These Streets Could Talk

"I have a list of names and if your name is called I ask that you exit the room and someone in room 113 will give you further instructions."

The first name they called was mine. "Giovanni Pizarro........."

I didn't hear any other names after that. I sat there in disbelief. I mean how are you just going to call people into a damned room in the middle of our shift and tell them that they don't have a job anymore? On top of all I'm going through I lose my job. I can't take anymore!

If you back a rat up against a wall he will come out fighting for his life no matter what the consequences and I was that rat. I thought God had forgotten about me so I had to look out for myself.

Back at home I contemplated for hours until I finally made a decision.

The next morning I put on my black sweat suit and black Timberland boots. I pulled my black ski mask from out of the closet and tried it on looking in the mirror making sure that it was still intact to serve its purpose. I went under my mattress and got my 9mm, made sure it was loaded, and headed down Center City on the train. On the El, I had to psych myself up. I wasn't going to let anyone or anything stop me.

When I got to the bank I had made up my mind that I didn't care who was inside. I was starving and needed to eat now. I was going after all of the money I could carry and if anyone or anything was to get in my way, I was going to kill it.

It was about 9:15 am, and the weather was bitter cold and dry. My fingertips were cold since I forgot my leather gloves while rushing out of the house to catch the morning train. I cocked my 9mm back and stuck it in the front of my pants.

If These Streets Could Talk

I looked around the streets at all of the business people on their way to work. Then that oh so familiar feeling that I get in the pit of my stomach when I knew trouble was about to occur hit me extra hard like I was going to shit on myself.

I peeked inside of the bank window to scope out the atmosphere. I noticed there was an old white security guard sitting at a table drinking coffee, reading a newspaper. I knew I had to take him down first since he was armed.

As I headed towards the door to enter the bank I felt my pager vibrate. At first I was going to ignore it but it alarmed three times in a row, which was odd. I snatched it from out of my pocket and checked the number recognizing that it was KK paging me 911 which she never did. I tried to disregard the page but her using code 911 broke my concentration. I knew it had to be an emergency.

I took a deep frustrating breath and rushed to the corner telephone booth to call her.

"Giovanni where are you at?"

"I'm over Yalanna's house KK, why?"

"Well get a pen and take down this number. That guy from the warehouse called and said he wants you to start work on Monday."

I started laughing in KK's ear as if someone were tickling me.

"What the hell is so funny about getting a job Bird Brain?"

"Nothin Mom, just give me the number please."

In a matter of seconds I went from doing a bank job to getting a real job. (My angel, I thank you again).

If These Streets Could Talk

Ch 29 The Lord Giveth. The Lord Taketh Away

I got a job working at a food distribution factory driving a forklift. I learned how to operate one after working in Jones uncle's lumber yard one summer.

I had been working there for about four weeks since the pay wasn't bad but the work was very strenuous. It worked for the time since I was just trying to get back on my feet but I knew I wouldn't be working there long. You know you have a hard job when at the beginning of every shift the foreman has everybody stand in a big circle and he leads a stretching routine.

It was about 3:00 pm and I had to be to work at 5:00 pm. Me and KK had our usual argument before work about how the kids were destroying my house.

"Mom I don't know how much longer I can take Maria's kids trashing my house like this. You know you can stay as long as you like but they have got to go."

Don't worry Gevonni I'll make sure I pay for anything they destroy, (knowing she didn't have any money)

"Have a good night at work."

She kissed me on my forehead as I left out the door.

When I got to work about one hour into my shift, my supervisor made an announcement on the loud speaker.

"Giovanni Pizarro, Giovanni Pizarro, please report to the office for a phone call." I had no idea who it was since I had never given anyone my work number.

When I got to the office I picked up the phone.

"Hello, who is this?"

It was Banita sounding hysterical.

"G hurry home! KK is having an asthma attack and she's barely breathing!"

I could hear Maria and her kids in the background screaming and crying.

"Banita, take a deep breath and calm down. Did you give her the inhaler?"

"Yes but it's not working."

" Ok did you call the paramedics?"

"Yea but they didn't get here yet."

Then I heard Maria in the background yell out.

"She's not breathing! She's not breathing!"

At that I slammed down the phone and ran out of the office. I heard my boss yell, "Hey, where in the hell are you going?" I just ignored him and ran as fast as I could to the parking lot.

My Mazda 626 maxed out at 140 mph but I think I was doing 150 mph. I was praying all the way to the hospital.

"Lord please take care of KK. I don't know what I would do if something were to happen to her".

When I broke through the emergency room door I saw all of Maria's kids in the waiting room crying.

"Where's Grandma?" I said out of breath. My oldest nephew Justin responded, "She's in the back with my mom, Aunt Banita, and Aunt Rochelle. They wouldn't let us go in the back," he said sadly. I tried to quickly console the kids. I pulled them all together for a group hug.

"Stop crying ya'll.

Grandma is going to be alright. I hugged them then headed to the back where KK was.

When I got to the room, I saw my three sisters. Maria was on her knees holding KK's hand. Rochelle was standing at the foot of the bed rubbing KK's leg through her blanket while Banita was patting her head with a damp rag. All three were crying.

KK had an I.V. and other needles and tubes running out of her hand and arm. Her eyes were closed but not as if she was unconscious but asleep. She had a sort of worried look on her face as if she wanted to wake up but couldn't. She also had a tube running from her mouth to a respirator, which was making her chest move up and down. It was the only thing keeping her breathing. I was in shock. Me and KK had just talked to each other no more than two hours ago and now she's hooked up to a respirator.

"What happened Banita?"

"I don't know. She seemed to be having an asthma attack as usual. I gave her the inhaler to revive her but she said it wasn't working."

Maria butted in, "Man she just fell in my arms and her eyes rolled up in her head. G she looked at me and said, "I'm not going to make it. This is it." Then Maria started crying as if she was reliving the moment.

Those words made me drop to my knees and burst out in tears and I mean hard like I did when I was a kid after a beating. I could never imagine KK ever saying she wasn't going to make it. She was too strong. She was a fighter and those were words of submission and I've never known KK to give up on anything. Especially on life.

Just then the doctor walked in. He appeared to be of Indian decent. He had jet black hair and dark skin. He wore thick glasses and spoke with a heavy Mid Eastern accent. He also had a very concerned look on his face.

Clearing his throat before he spoke.

"We ran several test on your mother and revealed that she lost oxygen to her brain for approximately 7-10 minutes leaving her in this coma-like state that you see her in. Rochelle interrupted, "Tell us straight up doctor, is she going to recover from this?"

He removed his glasses.

"I regret to say it but it's highly unlikely. That long without oxygen to the brain is severely damaging to the brain cells and when the cells die in the brain, they can't be repaired.

After hearing that we all cried for about ten more minutes all hugging each other. We had no idea what we would do without KK. She was our Queen Bee, our leader of life itself. And although we had other reletives we were never really close to any of them. She was all we had and all we knew.

Visiting hours were over in the emergency room so Maria, Rochelle, and Banita gathered the kids together and headed home. I stayed behind for a minute to be alone with KK. I took her hand and got on my knees.

"Lord please don't take KK from us, not yet. We really need her. She's the link that holds this family together and we're not prepared to lose her. I know your power Lord and I ask that you use it right know to heal my mother. She doesn't deserve this and neither do we. In Jesus' name I pray, Amen.

I stood up over KK and looked down at her.

"Mom if you can hear me I need you to wake up right now. Please don't even think about leaving me here with Maria and her kids."

I bent down closer to whisper in her ear.

" If you wake up I promise to make you a fat juicy steak. I promise."

The tears slid down the sides of my cheeks onto her forehead. I took a Kleenex and patted the tears away.

After not getting any response I just kissed her on her cheek and left the room.

For the next few days me and my sisters took turns staying with KK twenty-four hours around the clock. If she were to come out of this coma we knew somebody had to be there with her.

On the forth day all four of us were present when the doctor came in the room to check on KK. After he finished doing his usual tests to see if her condition has changed at all I followed him out of the room and pulled him aside.

" Be straight with me Doctor, is my mother ever going to wake up?"

"I'm sorry but like I told you before that her brain is severely damaged. And even if she were to come through she would most likely stay in this vegetable state that you see her in right now. She's not even breathing on her own. The only thing keeping her alive is the respirator. Now what you and your sisters are going to have to do is decide how long you're going to keep her on it."

I stepped closer to him and looked him in his eye.

"Honestly Doc, If that were your mother lying in that bed, what would you do?" He put his right hand on my shoulder.

"I'll put it to you this way. Science and technology are wonderful. We as human beings are more advanced than ever. Years ago there wasn't any machine made to breathe for people or medication to take away the pain. But in certain situations I really believe that man interferes with God's work. When they bought your mother in here she hadn't been breathing for a long period of time."

He then put both of his hands on my shoulders while removing his glasses then looking me dead in my eyes.

"I believe that God has already taken your mother's soul. All that's left here is a shell of what use to be. Honestly my friend, if that were my mother lying there, I would take her off of that machine and let God finish his work.

When he walked away his words were so sad, but so true.

When I went back into the room me and my sisters talked for about an hour and come to agree with the doctor. I knew KK wouldn't want to be lying in bed on display for people to see her in that condition. I also know she wouldn't want to live in a disabled state not being able to talk and walk around freely.

The next day we all had to sign some forms giving the hospital permission to remove the breathing tube from KK.

That evening the hospital allowed my entire family including Maria's kids in the room for the removal of the breathing apparatus.

We all gathered around the bed holding hands as the doctor removed the tube. Everyone in the room was crying except for me and the doctor. Maria and one of my nieces left the room not being able to watch.

I thought KK would stop breathing immediately when the doctor removed the tube from her throat but like I said she was a fighter. Surprisingly she coughed and began breathing on her own but remained in a coma. We all went home that night hoping God would perform one of his miracles on KK since she at least started to breath on her own.

The following morning during Banita's watch KK stopped breathing and all of our hearts were crushed. There is so much more to say about KK that I didn't share, but this woman was remarkable. She wasn't just my mother, she was my best friend. She had a heart of gold. She would give a total stranger her last piece of bread. And even though we made a lot of our money illegally, she has helped so many people save their cars and houses. She has bought milk for young mothers and has clothed under-privileged children. She has donated money and toys to abused woman shelters and would and have given a total stranger a place to sleep. Sort of like a female Robin-hood. But most of all she believed in family. Even when my sister was strung out on drugs or her kids were out of control KK continued to dedicate her life to taking care of them because they were family. Even when I needed a babysitter or just some advice or a listening mother's ear, she was always there for me. She impacted our lives so much that when I look at me and my sisters, I see a little piece of her in each and every one of us.

KK we love and miss you, but most of all we **thank** you for touching all of our lives in your own special way.

If These Streets Could Talk

Ch 30 Reassurance

After KK's death I went into a deeper depression. People always say they understand but only those of you who have lost their mother can relate to my pain. It's an indescribable emptiness that remains in your heart forever. Then to make matters worse, I got fired from the food distribution company forcing me to collect unemployment, which only lasted six months. After that I had no source of income at all.

Since I wasn't hustling anymore Yalanna would give me money from time to time to buy food and help me pay my bills but I couldn't keep up so I was forced to file a chapter 7 bankruptcy causing me to lose my house.

I refused to be totally homeless so I went back around the "W" and took all of the orange abandoned stickers and plywood off of the apartment building. I had my electrician buddy illegally wire up my building to give me electricity and my boy from the water department turn on my water, illegally of course.

I cleaned up the first floor and moved all of my belongings inside. I had reached an all time low. I was an official squatter. It made me feel like a real bum.

The day that I was moving my belongings into the "W" I heard the loudest car crash outside. When I went to the front door I saw my Mazda 626 totaled, then a gray truck smoking and speeding off. I mean the back of the car was pushed so far to the center that it was half it's normal size. It was a hit and run and I mean he hit it and ran. I was in total disbelief. I didn't have any insurance since I was out of work so just like that I was out of a car.

So many things were going wrong in my life the car almost didn't even effect me. I just cleaned out my glove compartment, locked the door, and went back into my apartment laughing to keep from crying.

During the summer time squatting wasn't so bad since I had a fan and air-conditioner. But when the winter hit, reality set in. No matter how many electric heaters I had I still slept in all of my clothes. It was too cold to take a shower so I would take bird baths from time to time.

My doorbell rang, it was Yalanna. When I opened it I stood in the doorway looking at her.

"Can I come in," she said insistently.

"Sure, why not." Hesitating not really wanting any visitors.

She came in and stood next to a chair since it was too cold to sit.

"G, I know that you're going through a lot but you have to snap out of it. I mean look at you. Your hair is wolfin, and when was the last time that you had a bath?" Waving her hand back and forth in front of her face.

I sniffed my underarms, "things smell OK to me."

"Well it's not ok. I know you G, and you like to look and smell nice at all times. Then she grabbed my left hand and looked me in the eye.

"Giovanni, you are a product of God."

At that I got upset and snatched my hand away from her.

" Look around here. I don't see or feel God's presence, do you? ."

She cut me off.

"See that's where you're wrong. The Lord is omnipresent. He's everywhere all of the time so you'd better watch what you say."

I sarcastically looked up, down, and all around the room as if I couldn't find Him. "Look. I didn't come here to preach to you, but it bothers me to see you like this. You're a fighter. You have KK's blood running through your veins and she never gave up. You also have two beautiful kids that need you and I need some help raising them. "Yea, well look around. I don't have nothing or nobody."

"See that's where you're wrong again. You have Jesus. G this might be a test of your faith and right now you're failing the test. Job 2:10 says: "Shall we accept good from God and not trouble?" Now don't get offended but every since KK died you haven't been in fellowship. You don't attend church anymore nor read the word. And when was the last time you prayed?"

"What's the point." I felt my eyes fill with tears. "I think my prayers get thrown in the prayer recycle bin anyway."

"Alright, can you at least do me a favor?"

" What?"

"Visit my church on Sunday because I think you will like it. It's a bible preaching bible-teaching church. It will give you food for thought."

I thought for a second.

"Are they going to pass the collection plate around ten times because I don't have a job."

"Don't be silly," she laughed. "We only have one tithe and offering during the service."

I hesitated Again, "alright, I'll go only in one condition."

"What's that?"

"You have to give a brother a ride. I don't have any wheels right now."

"That's cool. I'll pick you up at 11:00." She left my house with a look of excitement on her face.

Sunday came and Yalanna's church was huge. Compared to the one hundred or so members at my church they had a few thousand.

If These Streets Could Talk

The choir sang beautifully and like she said they only took one collection.

As the pastor spoke I wondered if Yalanna had told him some of my personal business because it felt as if he was addressing me personally. He talked about how we all are sinners and all fall short, but because God is faithful and just the bible says if we confess our sins and repent, he forgives us of our sins.

After that I started visiting Yalanna's church every Sunday until one day I was driven by the Holy Spirit to join. I felt my intimacy with the Lord growing stronger and the more I read the word; the more I desired it.

First, I was blessed with a job delivering medicine to senior citizens and saved up $1,000 to take to the IRS to make payment arrangements since they had threatened to garnish my wages if I didn't start paying back some of the $8,600I owed them for tax fraud.

When I got to the IRS building my friend Cheryl was still working at the front desk.

"Hey G, I see you're back," she said with a smile.

"Yeah but this time I have cash."

I patted my pockets.

"That's good because your Uncle Sam doesn't play."

I took a number and when she called my name I looked up and to my surprise I got chosen by Marcia Banks, the same drill instructor looking lady that handled my case the last time.

I followed her back to her office and sat down.

"Now Mr. Pizarro, what can I do for you today?" She sounded so insincere.

I cleared my throat.

" I believe I owe the IRS and I'm here to make some kind of payment arrangement."

She punched my name and social security number into her computer then a worried look came upon her face.

"There must be something wrong here," she said as she continued entering data into her computer. She typed and clicked her mouse several more times then looked up at me with a disappointed look on her face.

"According to our records you don't owe the IRS anything."

My face lit up with joy.

"Are you sure?" I asked with excitement. "There must be something wrong. I remember handling this case personally."

Then she stood up.

"Will you excuse me for a minute." She walked out of the office.

I immediately closed my eyes and began to pray.

"Dear Lord, please let this be one of your many blessings. I could sure use one."

As I finished my prayer she walked back into the room and handed me what appeared to be a receipt. She printed out a copy and gave it to me. I examined the paper very hard. It had my name, birth date, and social security number on it and at the very bottom in the far right hand corner there was a green box with a big beautiful zero in it. I couldn't believe it. My lawyer made it very clear to me that my bankruptcy would not erase my IRS debt or my water bill. I knew then it had to be the Lord.

Needless to say I walked away with my $1,000 in my pocket and in addition when I filed my income taxes for that year, I got a refund of $3,160. (Isn't God good?).

If These Streets Could Talk

Ch 31 You Reap What You Sow

After loosing custody of Ania, our biweekly weekend visits were too short and far between so I decided to take Marnissa to court to try and regain custody. I figured what could they do to me that they haven't already done.

The day of our hearing I was sitting in the mediation room waiting for Marnissa to show up for the hearing. Our meeting was at 9:00 am and it was 9:45 am and she hadn't called or shown up yet. I was a bundle of nerves not knowing what the outcome of the case would be.

The mediator, Miss Hill was a young blonde bombshell around twenty four or twenty five years old appearing to be fresh out of college. I could tell that she lacked experience by the way she would walk in and out of the room as if she were asking her superiors questions on what to do.

She tried to camouflage her lack of know-how by making small conversation with me while we waited for Marnissa.

"Mr. Pizarro I commend you for stepping forward in trying to take custody of your daughter. If we had more fathers like you our office wouldn't stay so crowded." "Well thanks for the compliment but I'm only doing what I know I should be doing. I've had Ania since she was three months old and my life is incomplete without her."

"Well I'm going to go talk to my supervisor and see what I can do to help you. You seem like a good man."

She left the room with a stack of papers in her hands.

I felt the need to pray so I closed my eyes.

"Dear God. You know my heart and you know I yearn to have my daughter back. I promise to be the best father I know how to be to her and if ever I feel as though I'm failing her, I promise to send her back to her mother.

People, I tell you no lie. At that very moment something came over me that had **never** happened to me before.

I felt an unexplainable feeling fill my whole body. The feeling started at the top of my head and slowly moved through my entire body to the very bottom of my feet then back to the top of my head again. It was a continuous feeling that riddled my body with goose bumps. I had once read a book by Joyce Myers where she had a similar experience describing it as being baptized in the Holy Spirit. I felt like I wanted to jump up and run around the entire room. I had to actually hold on to my chair to keep still. It felt so good I didn't want it to stop. It took all of my energy not to scream at the top of my lungs. After all, I didn't want Miss Hill to think I was some kind of psychopath or something.

Just then Miss Hill walked back into the room and looked at me kind of strangely. "Mr. Pizarro are you alright?"

The feeling started to subside a little so I answered her with a smile.

"Yes, I'm fine."

"Well I have good news. After discussing your case with my supervisors they concluded that since you've proved in the past that you're capable of taking care of Ania and the fact that her mother didn't even show up to the hearing, we're going to grant you full custody of your daughter again. Aren't you surprised?"

I just look at her and smiled again.

"I'm sorry Miss Hill, but I already knew.

I was at home looking through the help wanted section of the newspaper when my phone rang.

"Hello."

If These Streets Could Talk

"I hope you still have a bus pass because the streets aren't safe with people like you driving."

I paused for a second.

"Who is this?" I asked trying to recognize the voice.

"Do you have some candy G?"

Then it hit me.

"Sweeeeeeettttttsssss!"

She starting laughing.

"What's up G baby? I missed you."

I was full of joy, almost to the point of tears.

"Where have you been, where are you now, how did you get my number…"

"Slow down G, my cousin Trisha told me about KK's death so I finally got her to track down your number."

I tried to compose myself.

"Sweets I need to see you. Where are you?"

"I'm still living in Florida but Guess what G."

"What?"

" I got married and have a seven year old son."

I was astonished.

"My husband is away on business for three weeks and I always told him about you so he has no problem with you coming down to visit me."

"Well I don't have a problem coming to see you except I'm out of work right now so I can't buy a ticket."

"G don't worry about that, just give me your information and I'll charge you an airline ticket electronically."

Two days later I was in Florida with Sweets.

When I got off of the plane, her and her son were waiting for me with balloons and a sigh that read, "West Philly."

If These Streets Could Talk

Sweets was as beautiful as ever but I could still see the six inch scar that I permanently embedded on the side of her face from our car accident over thirteen years ago and her son was the splitting image of his mother. My first night at her house we sat up all night long talking and reminiscing about the old days.

Then every day afterwards, Sweets and her son treated me with nothing but pure love. She showed me all around Orlando and I didn't spend a dime, not like I had one to spend but she footed the bill everywhere we went. Case always said good things always come back to those who do good and he was right.

On my second day I was using Sweet's computer while she was at work thinking about my life. I started writing about some of my experiences when I noticed Sweets standing behind me reading some of what I was writing.

"G this is really good."

"You think so?"

"Yes, I'm telling you that it's really interesting. I'm going to leave you alone so you can give me more."

The following day I gave Sweets about ten more pages to read. I watched her as she read. She looked really interested in what I had written. She even laughed a few times.

"Giovanni I think you found your gift. You're a writer."

I chuckled.

"I ain't no damn writer, I hate writing."

"Well hate it or not you surely have writing skills."

She read some more.

"G, I do a lot of reading and you defiantly have what it takes to be a writer. She walked out of the room.

"I'm going to leave you alone so you can give me more to read.

If These Streets Could Talk

From that day on I've been writing this book. God has shown me one of my spiritual gifts through Sweets. We all have them. We just have to pray and find out what our purpose in life is.

Right now my life is on track since I decided to take the narrow road instead of the broad road as the majority of us usually choose. I don't look at Christianity as a religion but a way of life. I just try to live life by the golden rule: "Treat people the way I want to be treated." I've had several jobs that the Marine Corps assured I would never get because of my Bad Conduct Discharge, but little did they know that I am a child of God and only He can control my destiny. I've worked for the Government again with the TSA (Transportation Security Administration) and now I'm living my life long dream as a Philadelphia Fire Fighter. It's amazing how all I did was take from people and now God put me in the position to give my all to total strangers. When everyone is running out of a burning building, I'm running in. There's nothing more rewarding to me than helping someone in need. In all the jobs I applied for I never once lied on any of my job application. That's not a coincidence.

Presently I'm still growing spiritually. I'm not really where I should be, but I'm definitely not where I was. God has put a wonderful woman in my life whom I plan on marrying real soon. And I fell in love with her four lovely, happy, respectful children. I'm even blessed to say that Ania and Jamere are the first of my family ever to attend out of state college. I even wrote this book on nothing but pure faith.

I'm sure some of you can relate to what I am saying. Haven't you been in a circumstance or situation when harm or even possible death should have or could have come your way, but for some reason or another it didn't happen? In the movie "Pulp Fiction" Samuel Jackson called it "divine intervention." That's when God makes the impossible possible.

If These Streets Could Talk

All God wants us to do is worship him in spirit and truth and he will do the rest. He wants **all** honor and praise. For every one step we take towards Him, He will take two closer to us. He doesn't want you to worship money or entertainers or athletes as many of us do, (Luke 16:13). He is a jealous God (Exodus 20:5) and he will do whatever it takes to be worshiped. That's why when you're going through hard times don't always look it as a bad thing. It could just be God working on you to help you come closer to him.

Beloved people, I've done a lot of wrong in my life and it's all come back on me one way or another. All actions come with consequences and the decisions you make in life determine the consequences you encounter. This is my testimony. In life you reap what you sow. Let me ask you something. How do you sow?